DEADLY WEB

Christine Green titles available from
Severn House Large Print

Deadly Bond
Deadly Choice
Deadly Echo
Deadly Night
Fire Angels
Vain Hope

DEADLY WEB

Christine Green

Severn House Large Print
London & New York

This first large print edition published in Great Britain 2007 by
SEVERN HOUSE LARGE PRINT BOOKS LTD of
9-15 High Street, Sutton, Surrey, SM1 1DF.
First world regular print edition published 2005 by
Severn House Publishers, London and New York.
This first large print edition published in the USA 2007 by
SEVERN HOUSE PUBLISHERS INC., of
595 Madison Avenue, New York, NY 10022.

British Library Cataloguing in Publication Data

Green, Christine
  Deadly web. - Large print ed. - (A Kate Kinsella mystery)
  1. Kinsella, Kate (Fictitious character) - Fiction 2. Women
  private investigators - Great Britain - Fiction
  3. Detective and mystery stories 4. Large type books
  I. Title
  823.9'14[F]

  ISBN-13: 978-0-7278-7630-0

Printed and bound in Great Britain by
MPG Books Ltd, Bodmin, Cornwall.

One

As I watched flurries of snow begin to settle on the cars in the car park, a woman drove up in a four-wheel drive directly in front of my front door. I rushed to my office to get a better look at her from the camera monitors my landlord, funeral director Hubert Humberstone, had recently installed. Growing ever more paranoid, he assumes that I could be in danger one day from an aggrieved client. I run an investigation agency and I've previously been in danger, usually caused by my being a little reckless. Now, it seems, the combined efforts of Hubert and my boyfriend, Detective Inspector David Todman, are doing their best to dampen my enthusiasm. David wants to marry me, and I think Hubert holds a vague hope that one day I'll join him in the undertaking business. Neither scenario seems likely at the moment, although my agency is suffering from client famine, and one day I may need an escape route.

The woman's image on my monitor was grainy, but she stood staring at the sign on my door, which read *Kinsella Investigations*. Previously I'd confined myself to being *Medical and Nursing Investigations*, but as Hubert had pointed out, that did restrict my options and, thinking about my end – living above an undertaker's does make me think about my end – I didn't want an obituary that said: *Kate restricted her options*.

I waited for the doorbell to ring but the woman still hesitated. I had the urge to rush downstairs and pull her in. Something about her dress and posture suggested she was a country woman in despair. She was frowning and her shoulders were slightly hunched. She wore a green Barbour, a tweed skirt and brown knee-high boots. She seemed reluctant to ring the bell but eventually she summoned up the courage.

I quickly made my way downstairs to greet her. After all, she did look as if she could afford a PI. By now I'd already decided she was a long-married woman fearful her husband was playing away.

'Kate Kinsella?' she queried. Her voice was deep and, surprisingly, sounded full of confidence. The confidence, I thought, that usually comes with height and breeding, except that she was petite, not more than five foot two. I'd already decided that not only was she a 'marital', but that she was a 'horsey' type, mainly because a piece of straw poked out from the left shoulder of her Barbour. At my nod and smile of assent she said, 'I'm Mrs Rupert Decker-White,' as if her married name should mean something to me. I assumed then she thought he was someone important, because it's rare for anyone under fifty to refer to themselves by their husband's name. Mrs Rupert Decker-White appeared to be in her early forties and horse riding obviously kept her ultra-slim. Her dark, elfin-style hair had been only slightly tousled by the wind and snow, a sure sign, I thought, of an expensive cut. Tiny pearl earrings and a plain wedding band were offset by a diamond engagement ring set with a solitaire the size of a quail's egg. Her skin was in no way weather-worn and her nails were perfectly manicured, although unvarnished. I began to revise my opinion of her.

In my office, she sat down without being asked and took out her cheque book from a functional leather shoulder bag. 'You are my last resort,' she said, staring at me with eyes the colour of stewed tea. There was a touch of disdain in her voice which didn't endear her to me, but I smiled and said, 'What's the problem?'

'I'm sure you must have read about my husband's death in the newspapers.'

I racked my brain but Decker-White didn't register. 'I'm afraid not,' I said. 'Tell me about it.'

She raised an eyebrow slightly as if my ignorance was a slight insult. 'I'm sure you know my husband was a surgeon. He'd devoted his whole life to his patients and then...' She broke off and swallowed hard.

'And then what?' I prompted.

She paused. 'Someone murdered him. And I want you to find the person responsible.'

'What have the police found out?'

'They were worse than useless,' she said in disgust. 'They feel that after a thorough investigation – their words not mine – they can go no further.'

'How did he die?' I asked.

'He *was* murdered. I know he was.'

'How did he die?' I repeated gently. I was beginning to suspect that the grieving widow was slightly off kilter mentally.

'He was poisoned.'

'What with? What did forensics find?'

'Someone poisoned him by giving him something he was allergic to.'

'What was the substance?'

She looked at me balefully. 'Peanuts.

8

Everyone knew he was terribly allergic to them. He always carried one of those epi-pens of adrenaline, but on that night it was missing.'

'Surely it must have been accidental,' I ventured.

'No it was not! He was deliberately killed.'

'By a peanut?'

'I'm no fool, Miss Kinsella. I know it sounds improbable but I believe passionately that he was murdered.'

At that moment I didn't doubt her sincerity, but the anger of grief can make the bereaved look for causes and blame where none really exist. 'Call me Kate,' I said. 'And you are?'

'Victoria.'

'Did your husband die in Longborough?' I asked.

'No. He died at his private hospital in the East Midlands. I've driven over a hundred miles to see you.'

I was surprised, and I felt guilty, as I hadn't even offered her a cup of coffee.

I made her coffee and offered her my favourite chocolate biscuits. She ate three and while she nibbled I put her details on computer, although I was merely going through the motions. Hubert had been nagging me for ages to use my computer more.

Her address was The Pines, Longmore Lane, Upper Tapston. Rupert, aged fifty, had died at Fair Acres Private Hospital.

I looked up from the screen to ask, 'When exactly did your husband die?'

'He was murdered on January the first.'

'That was a month ago.'

'You're very quick,' she said sharply.

'Perhaps I should have asked you,' I said, 'why it has taken you so long to contact me. And why me anyway? Surely there are private investigators in the East Midlands?'

'Of course there are.' There was a long pause. 'If you must know, they agreed with the police – that Rupert's death was accidental.'

'Why should I think differently?'

'Because you're an ex-nurse and you could work undercover.'

I was a little taken aback, but thrust a biscuit in my mouth and nibbled away thoughtfully. An excuse came to mind quickly. 'I couldn't do that, Victoria,' I said. 'My registration has lapsed.'

'In that case,' she said, 'you could work as a carer.'

'Does Fair Acres Private Hospital need staff?'

'Most definitely – it's off the beaten track and, since my husband's death, a few of the staff have resigned.'

'I do have a major question,' I said. 'What makes you so sure your husband was murdered in such an unusual way? After all, he could have survived. Usually a murderer chooses a method that is fairly foolproof. Did he have any known enemies?'

'Of course he didn't have enemies,' she snapped. 'He was a fine surgeon.'

'And a fine man?' I queried. 'Because, if you're right, someone wasn't best pleased with him. Have you a suspect in mind?'

She shook her head. 'We'd only been married for three years. I thought we'd both found happiness at last. I was long divorced and he was a widower. He'd been working in Canada for ten years and...' She broke off. 'I'm sorry. I miss him so very much, sometimes I can't think straight.'

'Just take your time,' I said.

I needed time too. Murder by peanut allergy seemed tenuous to say the least, and the police obviously thought there was no case to answer, so what hope did I have?

'I would like you to take the case,' she said softly. 'Rupert was my best friend, lover ... my family. There is no one else. Not a soul.'

'Do you work?' I asked.

'Oh yes. I'm the financial administrator at Fair Acres. That's where I first met Rupert.'

No wonder, I thought, she knew there were staff vacancies. 'I'll have to think about it,' I said. 'I do have … other considerations.' I was thinking more of Hubert than David, and I needed to discuss it with both of them before subjecting myself to weeks of toil as a care assistant. Nursing is fine until you leave, then you realize there are easier ways to make a living. And you get scared thinking you'll make some ghastly mistake.

'Please,' she murmured.

I sighed inwardly, knowing that, if not today then tomorrow, I'd be saying yes. 'Is there anything you might have forgotten,' I said, 'or haven't told me about as a possible motive?'

She raked her hand through her hair. 'Just one thing,' she said quietly. 'He told me that when he was in Canada, every year near the first of January he received a postcard from England. It contained only two words – ONE DAY – in capitals.'

'Did you tell the police this?'

'Of course. They said it was hearsay evidence, as the cards had been destroyed.'

'And no further cards when he came back to England?'

'None.'

'So, for years there were cards, and then silence?'

12

'Yes.'

'It sounds as if whoever sent them died or simply didn't know he'd returned to England.'

'He had other post sent on but there were no more cards.'

'It's odd,' I said. 'But *"One Day"* doesn't really make a threat. Slightly sinister maybe, but since they've stopped being delivered, there isn't much to go on. What about postmarks?'

'Rupert said they were from all over the country.'

'An aggrieved patient maybe?'

'My husband was a wonderful surgeon.'

'All surgeons make their share of mistakes.'

She shrugged. 'Perhaps,' she agreed reluctantly.

'How did your husband ingest the peanut?'

'It was stuffed into a devil on horseback.'

'What exactly is a *devil on horseback*?' I asked.

Her scathing expression at my ignorance showed she thought I lived on burgers and fries. 'They are a canapé – a prune wrapped in bacon. They can be stuffed, but not with peanuts.'

'I see. Where did he eat this ... devil on horseback?'

'At the hospital's New Year party. It's

always a big event.'

'What about the cook?'

'She resigned once the police had finished their enquiries.'

I was nonplussed but intrigued.

'There is something else,' she said. 'Rupert was found by a staff nurse, dying in the surgeon's sitting room. She said his last word sounded like "Day".'

Two

By now, although I'd decided not to get involved, I was intrigued. One thing did trouble me. 'Were there any traces of peanuts found elsewhere in the hospital?'

Victoria Decker-White shook her head. 'No,' she said. 'I'd warned all kitchen staff that nuts were off the menu and were not to be used in cooking.'

Could this have been the perfect murder? I wondered. Had the police kept an open file on the case? Or even an open mind? There was of course only one way to find out.

'I'll have to think about it,' I said. 'At the moment I can't see that my listening to hospital gossip will solve a mystery that the police couldn't solve.'

She shrugged. 'I can't give up. I want justice for my husband.'

'Not revenge?'

'Yes, if you must know, I do want revenge. Someone took both our lives away.'

'Fair enough, but I'll need a day or so to

15

decide if I'm taking the case. And I have to warn you now, I think you may be wasting your money.'

She smiled wryly. 'Money is not a problem. I'm just hoping and praying you will be the one to find his murderer.' She paused. 'If you do decide to help me, please start on Monday. There is accommodation at the hospital, or there is a hotel in the village.'

I hesitated. 'If I decide to take the case, I'll stay at the hospital.'

Taking that as some form of acquiescence, she opened her cheque book and smiled properly for the first time, her face instantly looking far more attractive. The cheque she presented me with was generous. 'I will of course pay you normal care assistant's rates. Fair Acres doesn't do any major surgery – just the routine stuff – appendectomies, hysterectomies, stripping of varicose veins, hip replacements et cetera.'

I remembered then a nursing tutor saying during my training, 'Always remember a surgeon's "minor" surgery will be major surgery for the patient. Any surgery is potentially life-threatening.'

Victoria left, with my agreeing to telephone her within twenty-four hours, after I'd discussed it with my partner. Hubert would have been flattered to hear himself described

16

as such. If I agreed, I was to present myself at nine a.m. on Monday to the director of nursing – Louise Booth – who would show me around personally, as she did all new staff.

As she left my office, I couldn't resist removing the straw from her left shoulder. 'I live in the country,' she said. 'It must have blown in on the wind.'

I watched her as she walked briskly away. Now all I had to do was to tell Hubert.

Half an hour later, I walked Jasper and found myself, purely by chance of course, passing the baker's shop, which conveniently had a metal dog ring. Luckily Jasper enjoys watching passers-by, and always manages to look slightly pathetic, so he gets the odd word of encouragement and the occasional fuss. I took my time choosing two of their most expensive cream cakes. Clutching my beribboned box, I walked Jasper back, feeling both profligate and gluttonous, but I refused to feel one iota of guilt. After all, I reasoned, the media had induced fear about most foods, except for cream cakes, which were merely fattening.

Hubert found me in the lounge just after four p.m. 'You've been watching *Countdown*,' he said accusingly. Jasper had already left my side to greet Hubert with such excitement that Hubert had to pick him up and fuss him for several minutes. I won't repeat the endearments, because we can both embarrass ourselves, but Hubert's are always said in a loud voice, whereas I try to keep mine to mere loving whispers.

'You're only peeved,' I said rising from the sofa, 'because you weren't watching it with me.'

'Just as well I missed it. You know I always win.'

'Not always.'

Hubert, having just returned from his last funeral of the day, still wore his mourning gear, and not for the first time did I find that vaguely unnerving. Maybe I did need a change of scene.

'I'll put the kettle on, shall I?' he said pointedly.

'You know I'll make the tea. And I've bought cream cakes.'

'Been banking the calories, have we?' he asked as he left the room.

Living in such close proximity to Hubert, I'd realized for some time we'd fallen into spouse-like bickering and cosy-middle-aged habits. Such as watching *Countdown* together, having crumpets and muffins in the winter months at four p.m., cucumber sandwiches in the summer, and sometimes

18

having cocoa and chocolate biscuits at bedtime. Worse, though, was the fact that we repeated the same words and phrases, and each time I had a feeling of *déjà vu*. It wasn't a 'maybe' – I needed a change, I certainly did, I'd become comfortable, almost 'settled down'. David wanted me to 'settle down' with him, but I had no doubt he'd expect me to iron his shirts, find his missing socks, want me to warm his cold feet on my back and be grateful for sex. Hubert needed none of these things, and if I was honest, I'd begun to think that motherhood and keeping house might not be my forte. Also, the nearer I got to the big four-zero, the less I appreciated change. In fact, I was becoming scared of change. Unlike my mother, who globe-trots like a demented gypsy and views any degree of permanence as akin to decomposing. Even my ex-client and friend Megan and her toddler daughter Katy had moved away to a cheaper property in the Welsh hinterland.

Hubert came into the kitchen, dressed in grey cords and one of those zip-up cardigans, with Jasper hot on his heels. We drank tea, ate our cream cakes and kidded ourselves that the tiny pieces we fed to Jasper meant we'd hardly eaten half a cake each. Hubert, between bites, griped some more about the trend for Frank Sinatra's 'My Way' being played at every third funeral.

'I've got a new client,' I said in order to stop his grumbling.

'About time,' he said. 'Another marital?'

'No. This time it's murder.'

He picked up Jasper and began stroking him. 'Well?' he queried.

When I hesitated, he said, 'It's dodgy, isn't it? I know by the expression on your face you're worried.'

'I am not worried. It's just that I have to go undercover.'

'As what?'

'It's a hospital—' He didn't give me time to finish.

'You're not going to try to pretend to be a doctor, are you?'

'You can be really irritating, Hubert. I only have to pretend to be a care assistant.'

'Why not an RN?'

'My registration lapsed.'

'That's a pity,' he said. 'You won't earn as much.'

'Well, at least it will be hands on and not doing paperwork all the time.'

Jasper began to wriggle from his lap, and Hubert placed him gently on the floor. 'So you'll be snooping at the General,' he commented.

I hesitated. 'No ... actually, a place in the

East Midlands. Fair Acres Private Hospital.'

'You can't drive there every day,' said Hubert as if the matter was closed.

'I'll be living in.'

'How long?'

'However long it takes, I suppose.'

'And what about Jasper?' he asked, worried.

'The staff love him and they'll keep an eye on him while you're away.'

'Jasper will be very upset,' said Hubert avoiding my gaze. 'I think you're putting yourself out far too much.'

'You mean I'm putting you out.'

Hubert stood up and collected our plates and cups and saucers. Silently, his back towards me, he began washing up. 'I could crack the case in a week,' I said by way of cheering him up.

'Why haven't the police done just that?'

'It's complicatcd.'

He turned then. 'How complicated?' he asked suspiciously.

'The police think the victim, Rupert Decker-White, died from an allergic reaction to peanuts. So technically it was an accidental death.'

Hubert stared at me. 'That's not a technicality – that's a fact.'

'Not if he was deliberately poisoned.'

21

'Who says he was?'

'His widow.'

'Did he have any enemies?'

'She says not.'

'Don't touch it,' said Hubert. 'After all, if the police couldn't find anything, what will your blundering efforts achieve?'

More than peeved, I said crisply, 'A few weeks apart might do us both good.'

'Too true.'

I didn't see Hubert for the rest of the evening, but David rang later and he was equally dismissive. I wanted to say haughtily, *I wouldn't marry you if you were the last man on earth*. I didn't, I mumbled something weakly about it being a bit of a challenge and I might need some help. 'Don't rely on me, Kate,' he said. 'I'm off on a race relations course for a week, followed by another week's placement in Tower Hamlets with the drug squad.'

'You're always going away on courses,' I said, resentful that my new case was somehow sidelined as some irritating hobby. Also his remark, *'Don't rely on me'*, didn't augur well for a prospective husband. I was very fond of David, but I wasn't in love with him. My heart didn't beat faster when he was around, in fact nothing quivered at all. Perhaps my hormones were fading, I thought, and no man would be able to stir me again. On that depressing thought, I agreed to have dinner with him the following evening, hoping a few glasses of wine might help. A little pessimistic voice whispered in my head – *even a vat of wine won't do it.*

The following evening, after spending ages pampering myself, Hubert, instead of saying 'You're scrubbed up well' as he usually did, actually said, 'You look terrific.'

David was picking me up at eight and I was ready by seven fifteen, so Hubert opened a bottle of white wine and we sat, mostly silent, sipping and nibbling nuts, until Hubert took them away saying I'd spoil my appetite. At ten minutes to eight, David rang to say he couldn't make it. There had been a fatal stabbing in a village pub and he had to attend. He was most apologetic and, although I understood, I was miffed and disappointed and knew that, if I did marry him, that would probably be my constant state.

Hubert offered to take me out instead. I was wearing a decent pair of high heels and for once I didn't look like a typical dressed-for-all-weathers dog walker. Hubert's interest in feet and shoes is his only minor aberration and is totally harmless. It seemed a waste of effort not to go out, so I said yes, expecting him to take me to a local pub.

Much to my surprise, he took me to a new, expensive Italian restaurant on the outskirts of town. When he immediately ordered champagne, I guessed he was up to something.

'Kate...' he began as my eyes flicked over the other couples, who glimmered in soft candlelight and who seemed at that moment content in their coupledom. Hubert and I were definitely the odd couple. 'Are you listening?' he asked.

'Yeah, of course I am.'

'I want to talk about—' The champagne arrived at that moment in one of those silver buckets. 'What exactly are we celebrating, Hubert?'

The young waiter had thick black hair, eyes the colour of liquorice and lithe hips. He opened the champagne with a flourish, poured it for us, murmured something in Italian which I didn't catch and then winked at me. I watched him a little lustily as he walked away. I raised my glass. Hubert raised his glass too, but looked ill at ease. 'Just because I'm seeing David doesn't mean I'm not allowed to look at attractive young men.' I paused. 'Hubert, what's the celebration? Me going away or you being made Funeral Director of the Year?'

'I'm getting married,' he said.

My hand trembled so much that the champagne splashed on to the pink tablecloth.

Three

I put the champagne flute down and blurted out, 'But you can't be. You don't know anybody.'

'I do now.'

I could feel tears of shock and distress pricking at my eyes. I took a deep breath and a swig of the champagne. It tasted bitter in my mouth.

'I didn't think you'd be this upset,' said Hubert.

'I'm not upset. It just came as a huge surprise.'

'It's surprised me too.'

'Where did you meet her?'

Hubert's expression veered somewhere between guilt and glee. 'On the Internet.'

'*When* did you meet her?' I asked. Since he didn't go out in the evenings, I guessed he must have met her during the day. But I was still in shock. It was so unexpected.

With a slight shrug, Hubert muttered, 'I haven't actually met her yet. I've seen her photograph. She's very attractive.'

I took a sip of my champagne. I felt slightly relieved. 'Has she seen your photo?' I asked, trying to sound casual. 'I hope you sent her a recent one.'

'Not that recent,' he said. 'But I haven't changed much.'

'You haven't met her but you're getting married?'

'There's no need to sound like my mother – rest her soul.'

'Hubert,' I said, keeping my voice even and soft. 'Surely the initial meeting comes before planning the nuptials.'

'Our minds and souls have met. We have interests in common.'

'Such as?'

'She's got two hundred pairs of high-heeled shoes.'

'Oh,' I said, unable to think of a suitable retort to that gem of information.

'Her name's Shirley-Marie Baker and guess what?'

'What?'

'She's a qualified embalmer. You see, we met on a funeral director's website.'

I took a deep breath. It all began to seem real and serious. Hubert leaned over and patted my hand. 'Don't get upset, Kate, I'm sure you'll love her. And as soon as she gets her passport, she'll be over.'

'Where's she coming from?'

'The States. She's never been abroad before.'

'Has she been married before?'

Hubert looked up as the waiter appeared to take our food order. I picked up the oversized menu and decided uncharacteristically on sole and a green salad. My digestive system could just about cope with that. Hubert was obviously in celebratory mood, choosing lobster and fillet steak. This time I avoided looking at the waiter. I had far more important things on my mind. 'Has she?' I asked Hubert.

'Been married before? This will be her fifth. She's had a difficult life.'

'I bet she has,' I said.

'She was widowed twice and divorced twice. It's the way of the world.'

'It's obviously Shirley-Marie's way.'

'You're being a real bitch, Kate. You'll like her when you meet her.'

'The only person who *has* to like her is you. You're going to be the groom. When is the happy day?'

'We haven't arranged that yet. It's enough that she's said yes.'

Hubert took his wallet from his pocket and handed me a passport-size photo of his intended. I stared at her gaunt, unsmiling face. 'She looks so young,' murmured Hubert. He'd obviously got his rose-tinted specs on, so I merely nodded in agreement. I thought her face looked as stretched as the skin on a sausage, and her lack of lines gave her a corpse-like appearance, but if that was youth to Hubert, then who was I to argue? I just hoped she wasn't going to expect him to pay for regular Botox top-ups and further facelifts. Even so, he had money to spend, and perhaps she was *the* one for Hubert. I suddenly felt churlish for not being more pleased for him.

I handed back the photo and told him I looked forward to meeting her.

'I hope you'll get on,' he said. 'Nothing needs to change. She wants to work with me and she's heard so much about you that she's delighted you'll be on the premises.'

Our meal arrived and, although I'm sure it tasted good, I struggled over every mouthful. This change in my life was so unexpected that it made David's proposal seem like an escape route. That wouldn't be fair on either of us, and it seemed that I would have to review my whole life. I had some money in the bank and no debts. If push came to shove, I could re-register my nursing qualifications and work abroad, or set up another agency elsewhere. Both ideas scared me. I'd become comfortable and settled. And I was incredibly fond of Hubert.

'If you're worried about the future,' said Hubert, dabbing at his lips with his napkin, 'don't be. You'll be well cared for in my will.'

I swallowed hard. 'You'll probably outlive me, Hubert, and I ... don't know what to say.'

'Just you be grateful,' he said, sounding more like his old self. I'm not a complete old fool. If she's after my business, I'll know. And I'm checking her out. I won't be lost for things to do while you're away.'

Suddenly my foray into undercover work seemed a chance for me to look to my own future. I'd relied on Hubert too much in the past, now it was my turn to be independent, to manage an investigation without help from either Hubert or David. I'd crack this one alone, and if I couldn't, then I'd close the agency.

Later that night I rang Victoria to say I would take the case. We agreed that we'd pretend we didn't know each other, and she assured me that the Director of Nursing had been assured of my good character and nursing experience. Even as I put the phone down I had the feeling I'd made the wrong decision. After all, how much could I find out from casual gossip over a bed bath? The only saving grace was it would give me time to be alone and think. If my efforts failed to find murderous intent, at least Victoria might feel that she had done all she could to solve the mystery of her husband's death. Another bonus point being that I would be out of Hubert's way and less inclined to put a damper on his happiness.

On Sunday afternoon, Hubert helped me shift my portable television and two suitcases into the car. Jasper grew excited, thinking he was coming with me, but eventually my repeated noes sank in and he slunk away to his bed in a sulk.

I had the feeling that any initial doubts Hubert had harboured about my latest case had disappeared. He looked and sounded chipper. 'Don't eat any food you're not sure of,' was his sole piece of advice. Already I felt sidelined by the much married Shirley-Marie, but I smiled and waved and blew him a kiss – and above all hoped the USA would refuse her a passport.

The journey was uneventful, except that the traffic was heavier than I expected. It was growing dark by the time I pulled into the spacious tree-lined car park of Fair Acres

Hospital. I parked as near reception as possible and sat for a few moments surveying the scene. The landscaped grounds and ornate lamps gave the modern four-storey main building the look of a small hotel. Or perhaps it was the garish neon sign saying *Reception* that made it appear more hotel than hospital.

I left my suitcases in the car and walked into reception, which boasted rather dim uplighters and a fiercely red carpet. The receptionist sat in a leather swivel chair beside a computer at a dark mahogany desk. She studied the computer whilst I studied her. She was, I supposed, in her fifties, smart, in a grey suit and white blouse. Her short hair, although almost white, was thick and bouncy-looking. Her blue eyes paused from staring at the computer to look me up and down. 'Good evening,' she said with a broad smile. 'Do you have an appointment?'

'I am expected,' I said. 'Live-in staff. Kate Kinsella.'

The smile died. 'Oh yes,' she murmured. 'Care assistant.' The words *care assistant* were uttered in a tone that suggested *rat catcher* would have been preferable. I was neither patient nor anyone of status. The smile wasn't going to be resuscitated. 'I hope you haven't parked just outside,' she said crisply. 'There is staff parking round the back of the main building. The staff quarters are on the top floor. Please make sure the fire exit door is closed on your way up. And please note that this is a non-smoking building.' She handed me a set of keys with no explanation, and I noted her name badge read *Mrs Camilla Forsythe*. As I walked away I muttered, *'Bitch,'* once or twice under my breath and wondered just how disappointed she must have been with her life, when her name promised so much and she'd obviously peaked as receptionist.

I drove my car from the well-lit frontage to a dark and dismal second-class car park near the wheelie bins. There were two elderly cars parked there, and no one around, so I began lugging my suitcases out of my car. I pushed open the fire door and then saw that the stairs above were steep and poorly lit. I struggled upwards, pausing at each floor to recover. As I gasped for air like a dying fish, I resolved to use my time to lose some weight and get fitter – and, of course, if there was a murderer to be found, that too.

Eventually I staggered along the top floor corridor to find my room number four. There were three keys on the ring. Only the Yale would fit so that wasn't a problem. I hauled my suitcases on to the bed and looked around. The room was neat, clean, basic and bland, but it appeared to have everything I would need. My square box had magnolia walls, a single bed with a pile of bedding stacked on top, a bedside table and lamp, a sink and mirror, a pine wardrobe and a small dropleaf table by the reasonably sized window, the view from which was of the car park and wheelie bins, but further away were more trees and lawns.

I began unpacking and found the wardrobe had some shelving, so I could easily manage without a chest of drawers. I plugged in my radio and switched on. I was instantly cheered by the sound of voices, though I paid no attention to the content. The very thought of carrying up the TV tired me, so I decided I'd see how long I could manage without it.

Once I'd made up the bed and pulled the curtains, the room looked less bland. The duvet was a pale blue, matching the curtains, and I found the room quite soothing. Now that I'd unpacked, I soon became aware that something was missing, and I kept looking to the floor, expecting Jasper's warm body to be somewhere near my feet.

I rang Hubert's land line and his mobile. There was no reply, and suddenly I felt very lonely.

Four

After a few times of telling myself to pull myself together, I decided to go walkabout to find the bathroom and kitchen. Along the corridor was a locked door, presumably another bedroom. Next to that was the bathroom, a utility area with washing machine and tumble dryer, and then finally the kitchen. The bathroom had a standard white suite and the kitchen, although basic, did have a cooker, fridge, microwave and toaster. There was no one around to ask, so I decided to venture further and find out where the nearest shop or takeaway was situated.

I managed to find the internal stairs and, after one flight, I found myself outside Churchill Ward, near to a small sitting room where a depressed-looking woman sat in an armchair staring into space. 'Excuse me,' I ventured. 'You wouldn't happen to know where I could get a meal around here?'

'No, sorry,' she said dully. 'The kitchen is open until seven. Ask one of the staff.'

I walked along the corridor until I arrived at the nurse's station. There was still no one around. Planning to try the next floor down, I was on my way out when an older woman in a dark-blue uniform appeared from one of the rooms, looking flustered. 'Yes?' she said sharply. 'Can I help you?' She was a tall, angular woman with dark fine hair only half secured in a bun. Close up, I could see beads of perspiration on her frowning forehead. I guessed she was in her early fifties.

'I was looking for somewhere to eat.'

'Patient or visitor?'

'Neither. I'm a newly arrived care assistant.'

The nurse, whose badge read *Marie O'Grady – Ward Manager*, looked upwards and muttered, 'Thank you Lord.' Then, taking my arm in an iron grip, said, 'Come along, dear. I'll sort you out with food later. I need your help now.' She rushed me along to her office, took a white coat and a stethoscope from the back of the door and said, 'Put these on. I take it you're competent to take blood pressures?'

'Yes, I am ... but...'

'No buts dear. I've two theatre cases just back, both barely conscious. All you have to do is move between the two rooms doing their obs.'

I slipped on the white coat, stuffed the stethoscope into the left-hand pocket and took a deep breath. I'd thought, as a care assistant, I'd be bathing and toileting, not caring for post-op patients, especially on a Sunday evening. Marie hurried me along the corridor to the adjacent rooms. By the bed of the first patient, she said briskly, 'This is Damien Ole – footballer. He's had two wisdom teeth extracted and a knee arthroscopy. Keep an eye on his airway – he's been bleeding and his face is already swollen.'

Even I, a non-football fan, had heard of Damien Ole. A muscular, handsome Ghanaian, he was the football season's media hero, having scored two hat-tricks in two consecutive games – and having Angelina, a top model, as a girlfriend guaranteed celebrity status on a par with the Beckhams. A quick glance at him revealed swollen cheeks, a slack and bloody mouth, and he was snoring loudly. That's the trouble with nursing – heroes are all too human and vulnerable.

In the next room, a Mrs Monica Runcorn, aged forty-two, lay asleep following a hysterectomy. A quick glance at her observation chart showed that all seemed normal. I felt a bit calmer now that I had seen both patients, and when Marie rushed off to answer a call bell, I felt reasonably competent to look after them both.

I went back to Damien's room to find him beginning to stir and spit blood. I wiped his mouth, checked his pulse and BP, which were both fine, and gave him a mouth wash. I almost forgot he'd had knee surgery, but I had a quick peep under the bedclothes to check his dressing was intact and he wasn't bleeding. Opening one eye, he said huskily, 'Hello, darling.'

'Hello yourself. Have you any pain?'

He didn't answer, just closed his eyes and returned to sleep. I washed my hands and crept out to check on my other patient.

Monica was also conscious now, and asking for a drink of water. I did her obs and checked her dressing, then poured a small amount of water from the jug on her table into a plastic tumbler. After a few sips, she began to mumble and cry incoherently, but I did understand the gist. She wanted a baby and her childbearing days were over. I held her hand and wondered if anything I could say would be a comfort, then Marie walked in.

'Now then, pet,' she said firmly. 'You've got four lovely children. You needed that op – you'll be no good to them if you're not healthy.' Monica smiled wanly and closed her eyes.

Marie led me back to the office and presented me with a tray containing a plate of
sandwiches, a bowl of fruit jelly and a packet
of crisps. 'Best I could do,' she said. 'Just a
couple of favours before you go. We've had
two patients leave unexpectedly – could you
clean and make up the beds? The rooms are
on the right at the bottom of the corridor.
Bed linen's all ready.'

I nodded. 'You're not here alone, are you?'

She shook her head. 'Sometimes I might as
well be. My RN is with a terminally ill
patient. Open and shut surgery two days
ago. He's failing fast, continually vomiting.
There are two other carers on duty, doing
the routine stuff, but they are quite inexperienced and need a lot of supervision.'

She sat down to write her reports, and I
made my way to the empty beds. I'd just
finished making up the beds when I heard
voices along the corridor. I glanced at my
wrist, forgetting for a moment I was wearing
a fob watch. It was eight thirty and the night
staff were coming on duty.

This office was crowded now, with the
three staff I hadn't clapped eyes on, and
three night staff receiving the day report.
Silently I collected my tray and sloped off.
'See you tomorrow,' called out Marie.

Having found my way to the staff kitchen, I was just filling the kettle to make myself some tea when a slim, verging on thin, woman wearing a lavender uniform top and trousers appeared at the door. 'I'll come later,' she said softly. Her name badge read *Suki Kanda – Care Assistant*. I guessed she was from Thailand or Malaysia.

'There's enough water in the kettle for two cups,' I said. 'I'll make you one.' She glanced at my tray of food. Something in her expression told me she was hungry. 'I won't be able to eat all this,' I lied. 'Do you want to come to my room and share it?'

'I'd like that,' she said in the same soft tone.

Back in my room, we drank tea and shared out the food. I'd packed an emergency packet of chocolate biscuits and two yogurts, so all in all it was a bit of a feast. Suki didn't say much at first, but once she'd eaten she seemed to relax. 'You were starving,' I said. 'Have you been dieting?'

She didn't smile. 'We have to pay for our food, so I just try to have one meal a day.'

'You can't afford it?' I asked in surprise.

'I send my wages home to Thailand every month. My husband cannot work and my children cannot eat unless I send money.'

I felt really crass having mentioned dieting.

'How old are your children?' I asked.

'Six and eight. You like to see photos?'

'Of course.'

Suki rushed off to her room and returned with a scrapbook of photos.

We'd just sat down on the bed to look at the photos when there was a knock at the door – an urgent knock. I opened the door to a wide woman made to look wider by being dressed in a white towelling dressing gown. She'd obviously just been in the shower, as her wet hair still dripped. 'Is Suki there? I need to speak to her.'

Suki stood up, picked up her photo album and came to the door. I moved away and, even though the door was part closed, I could hear their conversation. The wide woman was saying, 'I need it now.'

Suki murmured, 'You had some yesterday.'

'It's today now. I've got to have it.'

'But you said...'

'I paid for it and I want it now.'

Suki sighed audibly. 'Come to my room – two minutes.'

The big woman's footsteps thumped down the corridor and then Suki pushed the door open further. 'I'm sorry about that. I have to go. See you. Thanks for the food.' With that she padded softly away. Her expression had been anxious.

I then lay on the bed and phoned Hubert. This time he was in.

'Cracked the case of the stray peanut, have you?'

'It isn't funny,' I said. 'A man is dead.'

'Point taken. What's the accommodation like?'

'Fine. The bed seems comfortable.'

'Have you found anything out yet?'

'Give me a chance. How's Shirley-Marie?'

I didn't really want to know. I was just being polite and trying to stop him from talking peanuts. The realization that I was on mission impossible had now fully hit home.

'She's great. With any luck she should be over here in less than a month. Just for a holiday at first – until we can finalize things.'

My heart sank. 'Oh good,' I said between gritted teeth. 'How's Jasper?'

'A bit clingy, but everyone is making a fuss of him.'

'That's nice,' I said. But it wasn't, of course. I wanted to be making a fuss of him.

We chatted for a few more minutes, mostly about the arrangements for picking *her* up from the airport. Her arrival now seemed inevitable, and although I felt a bit home-sick, at least I had a good excuse for not meeting her until I was ready. The difficulty of attempting to solve what could be a perfect murder might well keep me away from Longborough for some considerable time.

It was about one a.m. when I was awakened by the sound of a door being slammed and the sound of loud footsteps. I put my head under the duvet and thought of the wide woman and her desperate need, and I tried not to let my imagination run away with me.

Five

At nine thirty a.m. on the dot, I was outside the nursing director's office. The electronic sign on her door told me she was engaged, but I could hear voices anyway. A male voice raised in anger said, 'Your best isn't good enough.' I didn't hear her reply, but moments later a tall man in a grey suit rushed past me. The engaged sign stayed on for a few minutes, then disappeared. I knocked and a cheerful-sounding voice told me to enter.

Louise Booth was far younger than I expected, in her early thirties and very attractive. She wore a well-cut navy suit, pink blouse and high heels. Her blonde hair, in a fashionable choppy style, framed delicate features and liquid blue eyes.

'You must be Kate,' she said, smiling. 'Do take a seat. Welcome to the mad house.'

She picked up a gold pen and began filling out my application form. When it came to my recent nursing experience, I swallowed hard and told her I was living with my partner and helping him in his business. 'What type of business?' she asked.

'He's a funeral director.'

'Fascinating. Why would you want to work here?'

'Things are a bit rocky between us and I need a change.'

'I know the feeling. I've only been here a couple of years and sometimes it seems a year too long.'

She didn't elaborate but she handed over a brochure about the hospital, saying, 'In the private sector, everything must be individually itemized. If you give a client a few paper hankies or a paracetamol, it has to be on that client's account. It takes some getting used to, but we have to be meticulous.'

I smiled and nodded, trying to give the impression that I would be that meticulous.

'I'm sure you'll be an asset to us,' she said. 'But I hope you don't find it too hard to adjust to bedside nursing. The trained staff do seem to spend most of their time filling out forms.' She paused to put my form in a drawer and began to outline my pay and conditions. Then she said quietly, 'I have to warn you to be vigilant when helping to check or give out any medicines. Mostly this is the trained staff's responsibility, but often we have trouble recruiting the right calibre of trained staff, and we did have a problem with missing drugs a while back.'

I felt tempted to ask her about rogue peanuts, but instead I kept quiet.

'If you have any problems, please do come to me. We need happy staff, because happy staff means we have happy clients and our reputation stays intact.' She paused. 'On that point, you will find this place is a hotbed of gossip. Try not to get involved. Recently we tragically lost one of our best surgeons. His wife is our financial director and I'm afraid she's still in shock. She's on leave at the moment, she tried to come back to work rather too soon...' She tailed off as if distracted. Then, having collected her thoughts, said, 'Do you have any questions, Kate?'

As usual at interviews, I struggled to ask a single thing. Finally I managed, 'Which floor will I be working on?'

'Washington – named after a surgeon, not the city. It's on the ground floor. I'll show you round and introduce you to the ward manager.'

Louise did show me around the whole of the building, but at such speed I felt slightly disorientated. Each of the ward floors seemed fairly standard – ten single rooms with a nursing station in the middle, which afforded no privacy to the staff. I was obviously growing older to feel nostalgia for Sister's office – a place to moan or have a cry. There was a patients' lounge at the entrance to each floor, but at this time of the morning they were all empty. The staff seemed welcoming but harassed. Each floor either had a patient going to or coming from theatre. 'Our surgeons do have Health Service commitments, so much of our surgery is done "out of office hours",' explained Louise. 'And that puts a strain on the night staff, and means we need more staff rather than less at weekends.'

The theatre suite was situated on the floor beneath the staff rooms, and all three theatres were in use. The hospital kitchen was on the ground floor, and here I was allowed to peer inside. It sparkled with stainless steel and white goods. 'That's our new chef,' said Louise, pointing to a man with his back towards us, wearing chef's whites and kneading dough. 'He's brilliant. We're very lucky. And he bakes fresh bread every day. The clients here really appreciate good food.'

At the nursing station on Washington, I met the ward manager – Mark Alba. He was short, middle-aged, balding, had a limp handshake but a wide smile. 'We need you, my lovely,' he said. 'Don't be long.' Louise cast me a wry smile as we descended to the sewing room in the basement. 'It's no wonder I'm still single,' she murmured.

She left me outside the sewing room. 'Don't take too much notice of Doris,' she said mysteriously as she walked away. Even before I knocked, the door opened and there stood Doris. She was less than five foot tall, and if she'd been a pole dancer there wouldn't have been much of her either side of the pole. Doris, of course, was too old to be a dancer, pole or otherwise. A pair of rimless glasses clung to her over-large nose, and her face was a mass of wrinkles as interesting as a map. Short, thin grey hair had been clipped back, adding to her severe, thin expression. 'Another fat one,' she snapped. 'You'd better waddle in.'

I'm five foot four and still a size fourteen – just – but in comparison to Doris, I felt gargantuan. 'You can sit down,' she said. The room was small and windowless but well lit. Uniforms hung on rails against one wall, and in the middle of the room sat a sewing machine. There was a chair opposite the machine, so I sat down and hoped she wouldn't continue to be quite so insulting. As I looked at the strands of cotton littering the floor, I noticed she was wearing furry blue bedroom slippers. 'You'll have to wait until I've finished this alteration,' she said as she arranged the sleeve of a purple dress on the machine. 'That's the trouble with you young girls today. Greedy bitches, all of you. You eat too much, drink too much and fornicate too much.'

'Does fornication make you fat?' I asked, trying to keep a straight face.

'It does when you get wined and dined before you get screwed.' She began machining, her mouth set in grim determination. 'I hate doing bloody alterations. Every month this fat cow gets fatter, and I'm the one who has to try and eke out her uniform.' I had nothing to say to that, but Doris wasn't one to need a response. 'It's only the fat ones who stay. They like the food and the chocolates the patients give them. They take the mickey by bringing me boxes of chocs. I throw them straight in the bin.'

'You don't like chocolate?' I asked, although it was obvious that only the odd choccy could have passed her lips.

'I'm anorexic,' she said. 'Have been all my life. It's a miracle I'm still alive. Now then,' she switched off the sewing machine. 'Strip to your undies, and I'll find you a nice big uniform.'

I stripped off and she peered at me up and

49

down before handing me a purple dress. It certainly was big – it hung on me like a kaftan. 'You're deceiving,' she said, peering at me above her glasses. 'You're solid rather than fat.' Great, I thought. Doris really was an ego booster.

The next fitting was better. The dress nearly met my ankles, but according to Doris, sewing the hem would only take a few minutes. She placed a couple of pins front and back at the new hemline. 'You can't have it too short,' she said, 'so don't complain.'

Would I dare? She handed me a thin cotton wrap and I sat down to wait.

It soon became obvious that her sight was very poor. She struggled to thread the needle but was annoyed when I offered to help. 'I was threading needles before you were born, girl.'

'If it's not a rude question,' I began, 'how old are you?'

She fixed me with her beady grey eyes. 'If you must know, I'm eighty this year, and to be honest, I feel ninety.'

'Can't you afford to retire?'

A slight suggestion of a smile activated her mouth. 'I've retired three times but they keep asking me back. I only work mornings, and they can't find anyone else to do it. Girls these days can't even sew a button on. Years back, we made uniforms from scratch, but now I only do mending and alterations. It's surprising how much mending this place gives me – sheets, curtains, pillowcases, the pockets of the doctors' white coats – I do the lot.'

She continued to take up my hem very slowly.

'I hear one of the surgeons died here recently,' I said casually.

'Now *that* was a tragedy,' she muttered. 'He was a lovely slim man, so handsome and charming.'

'You knew him?' I asked, slightly surprised.

'I'd met him two or three times. I do a bit of private mending and a few alterations. I take that home. He had holes in the pocket of his favourite jacket, and a couple of pairs of casual trousers with weak seams. Years old they were, but I got the impression he was careful with his money. Rumour has it that he had plenty. Inherited quite a bit, I believe.'

'What about his wife?'

'Her!'

'You don't like her?'

She paused to break off the cotton with her teeth. 'I've only ever seen her once. She's the sort who thinks she's upstairs and the likes of us are downstairs. Mind you, it's only what I hear ... they say she's heartbroken, but I expect the money will make her feel better.'

'She gets the lot, does she?'

Doris was busy threading more cotton and she concentrated in silence. Once it was done, she continued sewing. 'What did you say?' she asked.

'Does Mrs Decker-White inherit all his money?'

'It's not for me to say. Some people just fall lucky. Others die tragically young. Like that poor girl that died.'

'What girl?'

'One of the nurses here. Could have been a model. Tall, slim – ever so graceful.'

'What happened?'

'It was November last year. Trina Brampton. Killed in a hit and run she was. Left a husband and a sister.'

'Where did it happen?'

'On the road to Little Makham by Finches Wood. Boy racers tear along there like maniacs. Nasty bends there are there. I should know.'

'You still drive?'

'I couldn't get here if I didn't drive, could I? My long sight is fine and I only drive in daylight. I know that road because I live in Little Makham. It's only about four miles from here.'

'Did the police find the driver?'

'Oh yes. Seventeen years old. He'd just passed his test and couldn't wait to get his own car, so he borrowed his dad's. He denied it, of course – little sod.'

'How could he deny it?'

'He said he didn't see her car at first, because its lights were off and he thought it was abandoned...' She tailed off. 'Well, anyway, after running her over he just drove off.'

I did wonder if Doris had glossed over quite a bit of information, but as she began to gnaw at her last piece of cotton, I decided I could always find out more later. 'There you are,' she said. 'All done. You can get dressed now.'

The purple dress *was* too long, but I had no option but to wear it, as I was due on Washington Ward. 'Lose a stone, dear,' said Doris. 'Then I'll be happy to alter it for you. The colour suits you. I'll get two more ready for you when I can.'

As she opened the door for me, she said quietly, 'You take care, dear. Believe me, this place is jinxed. Keep your wits about you.'

Doris might be old and odd, but I *did* believe her.

Six

By the time I arrived on Washington Ward, I'd expected most of the morning's work to be over. Instead the place seemed in chaos – trolleys passed each other going to and coming from theatre. Walking patients had to accompany a trolley patient and share an escort nurse. The lifts were buzzing frantically, and in the midst of all this, one of the domestic services staff was trying to negotiate her trolley to deliver the mid-morning drinks.

I managed to track down Mark the manager in the clinical room, standing by the open medicine trolley. I stood in the doorway as he rattled off irritably, 'I've just finished the ten a.m. drug round and in twenty minutes I'll be starting the twelve a.m. round. I'm an RN down. She's got the bloody flu. Anyone else has a cold and soldiers on, but not her – she has to be off for at least a week. And what kept you?'

'Doris.'

'Doris the old crone. She's the "ist" in most words – fascist, sexist, *fat*ist and a fatalist. She's the voice of doom.'

'She's harmless though, surely?'

Mark shrugged. 'Maybe ... Anyway, to work – two rooms, four and six, need the bed cleaning and making up. The patients are in the day room waiting for collection like parcels. When their relatives come, escort them down to reception. Rules are, a care assistant must accompany them off the premises – just in case they take a tumble and decide to sue. Between you and me, half of them aren't fit to go home, but the money is in the surgery and not the aftercare.'

I hurried along the corridor and felt a certain relief at being in an empty room. I didn't dawdle though, and quickly moved on to room six. The rooms were comfortable but small, although they did have an en suite shower and loo. They reminded me of cheap hotel rooms, with the angled television on the wall and no sense of individuality, except, of course, for the smell left behind. In this case it was Chanel No 5.

After accompanying Mark on the medicine round and helping three patients back to bed, I was sent to lunch. I hadn't been shown the staff cafeteria, but I was assured it was next to the kitchen. And indeed it was.

Squashed in and very poky, I supposed it could seat about twenty. It reminded me somewhat of Hubert's catering suite, but with no hint of pink and grey, although the pale-green tiled floor and green chairs were subtle enough, and a few fronded plants lent the place a continental air not matched by my first sight of the food.

I stood in the queue, tray in hand, with two strangers in front of me and a glimpse of a white coat behind me. The hot food already looked tired, but the salads covered in cling film looked even sadder. I must have been dithering, because a white coat behind me murmured in my ear, 'Go for an omelet. They make them to order – they're great. I have one every day of the week.' I turned, expecting to find a nerdish type. Instead the guy was a slim Asian with eyes like liquid coal, thick black hair and a set of features nigh on perfect.

'With a recommendation like that, I'm game,' I said, giving him what I hoped was a come-hither smile. I ordered my omelet and was told by the large red-faced woman who doled out the food that it would be delivered to my table.

Choosing an empty table in a corner by the wall, I had a good vantage point for the whole place, and was delighted to see the omelet man walking towards me. 'Mind if I join you? We can wait together.'

'I'm glad of the company. I'm new.'

'What brings you here?' he asked.

I hesitated, not because I didn't have an answer, but because I was mesmerized by his eyes. Eventually I muttered, 'Sorry, but you do have extraordinary eyes.'

'I should have been a hypnotist then, instead of an anaesthetist.' He smiled, showing perfect white teeth.

'Back to your question,' I said. 'I came because I needed a change of scene.'

'Are you married?' he asked.

I shook my head.

'I guess you're fussy,' he said.

'Probably. What about you?'

'I'm engaged. Getting married next year.'

'I'm Kate. You don't sound too happy about it.'

'I'm called Rav, real name is Ravinder Singh Ghopal, and let's just say our families think we are the perfect match.'

'And you don't?'

'She's a doctor and very career-minded...' He broke off as our omelets arrived.

We fell silent for a while. Rav was short for ravishing, for he was very handsome, but like most attractive men who pass my way, he was spoken for and best avoided in the future.

The omelet was delicious, but it did remind me of the real reason I was here.

'Did you know the surgeon who died at the party?' I blurted out. Being subtle is obviously an asset to someone working undercover. I'd have to work at it, because he did look surprised at the question.

'I was at the party,' he said. 'It was a real shock. Everyone knew he was allergic to peanuts, but there were no nuts of any sort to be seen.'

'Did you actually see him die?'

'No. It seems he died in the kitchen. No one knows why he was there. The police questioned everyone at the party, but to be blunt, most of them were so drunk he could have died ... at this table ... and no one would have noticed.'

'But you were sober?'

'I was on call. I couldn't risk having a drink.'

'Did you like ... what was his name?'

'Rupert. He was a good surgeon. Inclined to panic occasionally, but very pleasant.' He stared at me for a moment with slight suspicion. I was obviously asking too many questions. The mobile phone in his pocket saved the day by trilling the funeral march, which proved to me he was a man with a sense of humour. 'Must go,' he said. 'See you.' As he rushed away, I wondered if I'd rattled him with my questions, or was he merely making a hasty escape from me?

Back on the ward, the patients were having their rest after lunch, and a hush had fallen. Mark introduced me to an RN, Polly Waters, who would go through the fire regulations with me, and the crash call system. Once Mark had gone off for his lunch, Polly showed me where the fire extinguishers were on the ward, and how to deal with the fire alarm system. Polly was as perky as her name. She was probably in her mid-twenties but looked nineteen, with her straight blonde hair in a ponytail, a trim figure, a perfect tan, and far too pretty to need make-up. Her accent, I guessed, was Australian. 'Time for a smoke,' she said. 'There's two HCAs on the floor – they know where I'll be.'

I'd seen one young health care assistant at the nurse's station and, as we walked past, Polly winked at her. In the sluice room, Polly opened a window wide and took out cigarettes from her pocket, offering me one. I shook my head and she said, 'I'll give up when I'm thirty. Thirty sounds so bloody old, doesn't it?' She sat on the stainless-steel sink and puffed her smoke out through the open window. 'How long have you worked here?' I asked.

'About a year,' she said. 'I'll be moving on soon. I haven't decided where yet.' Then she said, 'You got a fella?'

'Sort of,' I said.

'Brit men are a pain. Like Aussie men, only more childish. All I seem to meet are wackos and nerds.'

'Or they are already taken, like the gorgeous Rav.'

She laughed dryly. 'Take no notice of that. I've been told he's been engaged for years. It's his way of keeping women at bay.'

'Still hope for me then,' I said. She took a long look at me, then blew smoke out of the window before saying, 'I've heard he likes older women.' I felt a little crushed. I was older than him, but I didn't feel it. On the inside I was still twenty. It was time to change the subject. 'What about the surgeon who died at the party?' I asked.

'Poor Rupert. Great bloke, he was. Really attractive for an old guy.'

'Were you at the party?'

She smiled. 'I think so. I can't say I remember much. By midnight I was so boozed up – it's all a blur.'

'His poor wife,' I murmured. 'She must have been so shocked.'

'Yeah, but she was as pissed as the rest of

us. She hadn't let the poor bugger out of her sight. She clung on to his arm like a demented chimp.'

'I thought he was found in the kitchen on his own.'

'Yeah, somehow he slipped the leash and landed up dead.'

'So the police broke up the party?'

'The police?' she queried. 'I didn't see any police. Some people didn't know anything had happened. It seems someone injected him with adrenaline, gave him oxygen and CPR, and then an ambulance came and whisked him away.'

'What about the party?'

'It...' She broke off as the pager in her pocket buzzed. 'Bloody thing,' she said, taking it out and staring at it. 'These are new. Just for the RNs at the moment. It's a way of making sure we answer the call bells quickly.' She ran her cigarette end under the tap and threw it down the sluice sink, flushed it away and then squirted air freshener liberally in the air. 'It's room five. Mrs Akers. She probably wants help getting out of bed. I'll need a hand – she weighs a ton.'

Mrs Akers, in fact, wasn't planning to move at all. She lay in bed clutching her chest, having difficulty breathing. Her face was ashen and her lips turning blue. 'Pain in my chest ... I can't breathe,' she gasped.

'This will help,' I said as I attached the oxygen mask to her face. I took hold of her pudgy hand and told her she would be just fine and that the doctor was on his way. Her eyes watched me fearfully. Polly, meanwhile, had paged and phoned for a medic. It seemed that we waited for ever, but it was probably less than ten minutes. Polly had taken her blood pressure and we tried to sit her up to improve her breathing. Then she rushed out for the ECG machine and IV equipment.

When the doctor did arrive, he looked young, inexperienced and worried. He wore glasses and his dark hair was overlong and greasy looking. 'Where the hell is the ECG machine?' he yelled.

'Right behind you,' said Polly calmly.

'I'll need to get an IV going and do bloods.' Then, as if remembering Mrs Akers was a human being, he said, 'Now just relax and breathe normally.' The word *relax* must be the most overworked word in the medical and nursing profession, said by those who have never been fearful or in pain. Mrs Akers clutched at my hand as if she were drowning. At that moment, Mark appeared. I was relieved and I even sensed that Mrs Akers too sighed with relief. Polly obviously wasn't that experienced, and the doctor, whose name badge read *Giles Forbridgeworth – Resident Doctor*, appeared only just old enough to be qualified.

Mark quickly took control. 'Kate – you go back on the floor and do the two p.m. obs. And Mr Davis in room one needs help.'

I went straight to room one and Mr Davis did indeed need help. He was an elderly man, tall and thin and very distressed that he'd 'had an accident in the bed'. I was very matter of fact, telling him it happened all the time and he was in the hands of a true expert. He managed a wry smile.

A short time later, when he was dressed in clean pyjamas and propped well up in a clean bed reading his paper, I thought that no matter how high-tech nursing gets, nothing quite beats the satisfaction of providing the comfort of basic nursing care.

Doing the observations with a care assistant called Alice Carne proved to be a bit of an education. Middle-aged and obviously menopausal, she had to stop to fan herself every few minutes with one of those pocket-sized electric fans. That didn't stop her having an opinion on everyone and everything. Outside each door, she would give me the lowdown in her own graphic language. PC in her world only stood for police constable. We'd started in room ten. 'Spoilt bitch, this one. Wears a cashmere cardie in bed. Can you believe it? I think her old man is a judge. He's a real old fart – kisses her hand all the time.'

By room four I was growing weary of her constant carping – I'd been lectured on 'bloody foreigners', 'rich bastards', 'perverts' – that category included gays, lesbians and paedophiles – 'do-gooders' and 'mealy-mouthed, lying politicians'. When we passed Mrs Akers' room, Alice went a tad too far, saying Mrs Akers was 'a soppy fat cow who treats her dog like a baby'.

'Alice,' I said crisply. 'You are really getting on my nerves. Don't you ever stop?'

'Having a moan keeps me going.' Her mean little mouth pursed as she fell silent, and I suddenly recognized in her tight little features and thin greying hair the animal she reminded me of – a ferret. All I know about ferrets is that some people keep them as pets and they are prone to travel up trouser legs, but Alice could be useful. I certainly didn't want her as a friend, but then, neither did I want her as an enemy, and undoubtedly, when in need of information, who better than a human ferret?

'Alice,' I said. 'Did you go to the New Year party?'

Seven

'Wouldn't miss that,' she said. 'I've been to every one in the last ten years.'

'So Fair Acres parties are pretty special?'

'I enjoy them,' she said slyly. 'I watch their smug faces and see them getting legless. What could be better?'

What indeed, I thought. I was about to ask her more, when Mark appeared. 'Stop gassing, Alice. Mrs Akers is being transferred to the General. Seems as if she's had a mild heart attack, but our consultant physician, Mr Mahmood, wants her with his cardiology team, so go and pack her things. You can go with her. And watch your language.'

'I'm not a hypocrite – like some,' she retorted as she flounced down the corridor.

Mark raised an eyebrow at me. 'Come to the nurse's station,' he said, 'and I'll show you the paperwork for patient transfer.'

Once we'd sat down he said, 'Don't take too much notice of Alice. I know she's all mouth, but strangely the patients seem to like her. And she does have a tragic background.' He began pulling out forms from drawers. 'She's been with us since this place was opened ten years ago. The nursing director at the time was married to a senior social worker, and he persuaded her to give Alice a job. She'd been treated for severe depression following the loss of her three children, her husband and her mother in a house fire. She'd been working nights and she arrived home to find her whole life destroyed. She's never been the same since.'

I wasn't surprised. 'Does she live alone?' I asked.

Mark shook his head. 'She tried but she couldn't cope. She lives in a community home. They're very good to her. One of the social workers drives her to work and picks her up. The one thing you do have to be aware of with Alice is the sound and sight of fire engines. Burnt toast causes a few call-outs each year, and if she's on duty she gets into a terrible state. So be warned.'

Having shown me the paperwork, Mark told me to help Polly with the meds round, which by now was running very late.

Polly seemed pleased to see me, and we raced round doing the meds, although by now visitors had begun arriving, bearing flowers and requests for tea. 'Most of the patients are great,' commented Polly. 'But the visitors are a pain in the butt. After all, it's not a bloody hotel.'

The afternoon progressed, and I left the floor just after five, as the evening shift arrived. It was only when I got to my room that I realized how tired I was. One day's nursing and I was knackered. I stripped off my uniform dress, put on my dressing gown and lay on the bed and stared at the ceiling. The first day is always the most tiring, I told myself. New faces, new information to take in, even the geography of the building caused me sensory overload.

Outside, I could hear cars arriving and leaving, then a scattering of rain at the window, and finally I heard nothing at all.

When I did wake from sleep to the sound of my mobile, I was disorientated, not knowing if it was night or day. I glanced at the windows, only to see the rain beating at them against a black sky, and I was still none the wiser. I peered at my alarm clock. It was six thirty. I grabbed the phone from my bedside table. It was Hubert.

'Is it day or night?' I asked.

'You don't change, do you?'

It wasn't a question.

'It's p.m.,' he said. 'Your name is Kate...'

'I'm not in the mood. I've been sound

asleep and I'm still groggy.'

'Have you been drinking?'

'I've been working,' I snapped.

'Ah well, that explains it.'

'Very funny.'

'Do you want me to ring back later?' he asked.

'No. Just bear with me. I'll have a few swigs of Diet Coke.'

I staggered off the bed and found a half-full bottle of Coke. I drank the lot and it did help.

'How are you, Hubert?'

'I'm fine and dandy.'

He did sound cheerful, so I reasoned his great romance must still be a goer. I waited for him to say more but he didn't. Somehow I couldn't bring myself to ask about *her*. Instead I asked about Jasper.

'He's missing you.'

'He's not fretting, is he?' Suddenly I wanted to leave this place and drive straight home. I could be back in two and half hours.

'No, don't worry. He's eating well and sleeping, but occasionally he searches for you.'

'I'll be back on Thursday evening. I've got Friday and Saturday off.'

'It's very quiet without you here. I'll cook you something special for Friday. Now ... tell me what you've found out.'

'I've only been here a day. Give me a chance.'

'Don't get on your high horse. I bet you've got a theory.'

'Well, I haven't, but you could do me a favour – see if Rupert Decker-White is listed on the Internet.'

'I'll do my best.'

A sudden wave of homesickness made me say, 'I don't like it here. I think it's a bit sinister. My client Victoria has gone on sick leave for some reason. She seemed to be coping before.'

'That's not sinister. She has recently been bereaved. Maybe you being on the premises means she can grieve, knowing you're doing your best on her behalf.'

'It's not just that. It's...' I struggled to put into words how I was feeling. 'I suppose there seems to be a lot of death around.'

'Not murder?' asked Hubert in surprise.

'No. Accidental deaths. One recently. I'll tell you all about it when I see you.'

When Hubert rang off, I felt slightly cheered, although I couldn't stop myself looking on the floor for Jasper, in case I stepped on him. It was a hard habit to break, because if Hubert wasn't around, Jasper was always close to my feet. Technically Jasper was

Hubert's dog, but my feelings for the little scrap were so strong I was willing to fight for him, and at the very least expected shared custody.

In a deep hot bath I mulled over the day, my future and Jasper's, and gradually the bath relaxed me enough to allow thoughts of an evening meal. I would go out, I decided, and find a decent pub that served food. I must have been in the bath for half an hour when someone banged on the door. It wasn't Suki, I was sure of that – the bangs were too loud and aggressive. 'Give me two minutes,' I yelled. Silence. I towelled myself dry quickly, slipped on my dressing gown and opened the door. There stood the wide woman, but this time she was smiling. 'Sorry to rush you, but I'm going out. I'm Lorna Berry, by the way. I'm the RN on Toronto.' Whatever she'd been wanting the previous evening, having it had done her the world of good. I introduced myself and then, to my surprise, she said, 'Suki's off this evening and we're going out for a meal. Do you fancy coming with us?'

'Great. What time?'

'I've booked a taxi for seven thirty. We'll give you a knock.'

Back in my room, I decided to wear jeans with heels and my favourite black top. I

70

decided that, next to Lorna, I'd appear quite sylph-like, but next to Suki I'd look broad in the beam. That's life, I told myself, and now I was in my thirties, I was reasonably content with the way I looked. After all, it was downhill all the way from now, so I should make the most of it.

The taxi was waiting for us in the car park and we piled in. Suki looked like some delicate oriental flower, with her hair secured high on her head with a butterfly clip. Lorna wore a black skirt and a voluminous black top. She wore a slick of lipstick and seemed quite animated, although she was moaning about the computer system on her ward. Suki smiled shyly at me and sat in tranquil silence for the ten minutes it took to get to the Red Lion pub.

Lorna had booked a table in the restaurant section, and the manager and our waitress knew her by name. It was one of those pubs with a huge salad cart and a placard endorsement to 'Eat as much as you like'. Our table was the nearest to the salad cart. Lorna ordered a bottle of red and a bottle of white wine and eyed the menu as lustily as a man with a pornographic magazine. When the young waitress urged us to 'help ourselves', Lorna had managed only a sip of wine before rushing across to the salad cart and busily filling her bowl. Suki murmured, 'Lorna loves her food, she just doesn't love life enough.'

Lorna returned with a huge pile of 'salad' and two bread rolls. On top of her food was a mound of mayonnaise covered with croutons. 'Go and get yours then,' she urged. Suki chose a little pasta and cherry tomatoes. My choice was varied, but I felt virtuous forgoing the mayonnaise. Neither of us had a bread roll. By the time we returned to our table, Lorna had nearly finished. 'That was nice,' she said. 'But I'll need some more.' Moments later, she got up to refill her bowl. Suki shrugged, 'I try to help her, but it's not working. She weighs eighteen stone – that's very big. Bad for her heart.'

When the main course came, Lorna had consumed two bowls of 'salad' and ordered lasagne with garlic bread and a bowl of chips on the side, but by now she was a lot more cheerful and talkative. 'What brings you to this neck of the woods, Kate?'

'My partner seems to have found another woman on the Internet.' That was true, but I took twenty years off Hubert's age, called him Steve and made out he was a complete babe magnet.

'Bastard!' proclaimed Lorna. 'My ex-partner was even worse. We'd lived together for five years. The day before the wedding, he did a bunk with my car, my credit card and cash. He'd filled the car with half our household goods and left me with a mortgage I couldn't pay. The police haven't been able to find him, and he cleared my bank account before I could stop use of the card. I think he's gone abroad.'

'So that's why you live in?'

'Yeah. I've been at Fair Acres for two years. I've saved a bit, but I'll only ever be able to rent. At the moment I'm OK in my little room.'

Suki smiled, 'I like my room, but I would rather be at home. My husband, Don, is a cripple, so when the chance came to come to England, I took it. My young sister looks after Don and the children, but the money I send back helps her too.'

'We're all lost souls, aren't we?' I said.

Lorna smiled. 'That's true, but you don't have an eating problem. I wasn't always this weight. I used to be slim and attractive. I just can't stop eating. Rupert Decker-White, the surgeon who died at the New Year party, was going to operate on me – put one of those bands around my stomach. He was going to do it for free, but he died, so that's that.'

'I heard about that,' I said. 'Someone told me the police were suspicious about the circumstances.'

'They questioned everyone who was at the party,' said Suki.

Lorna's eyes had begun to fill with tears. 'Take no notice of me,' she said. 'I was the one who found him.'

Eight

'What happened?' I asked, just as our main courses arrived. At the sight of her lasagne, Lorna's eyes widened and I knew I'd have to wait for a while for any details. She began to eat fast, almost manically, until Suki put down her knife and fork, touched Lorna on the arm and said softly, 'Slow down. Take it easy.'

'Sorry,' murmured Lorna. She smiled at Suki and again her eyes were filling with tears. 'Suki's trying to help me. She keeps a stash of chocolate and biscuits in her room, and then doles some out to me when I'm desperate.'

Suki gave a little laugh. 'You're always desperate – every day.'

Lorna began to eat more slowly then, but I waited for a few minutes before broaching the subject of her finding Decker-White.

'I found him on the floor in the kitchen. He was barely alive. I yelled for help but the music was loud and no one heard me. I rummaged in his pockets for his epi-pen but it wasn't there. His lips were swelling up and he was obviously choking to death. I started to scream for help and then he stopped breathing. I did CPR and suddenly people came rushing in. Someone gave him adrenaline but it was too late.'

'Did he manage to say anything?' I asked.

Lorna gave me a strange look. 'I can't be sure, but it sounded like "day" but it could just have been air being expired – I don't know.'

'What about his wife?'

'She came in when it was all over. Someone had called an ambulance by then, and Louise, the director of nursing, had run off for an oxygen cylinder, but it was all too late.'

'So he went off to the General?'

'Yes, eventually. The ambulance took more than half an hour to arrive.'

'What about the police?'

'They didn't come until the following day. It was me they questioned the most.'

'What did they ask you?'

'Mostly about his epi-pen. It seems it was only a few feet away from him, but I didn't see it. I feel it's my fault he died. I'd drunk such a lot that night.'

Suki patted her hand. 'You did everything

you could. It wasn't your fault.'

'Was there a post-mortem?' I asked.

Lorna nodded. 'Oh yes. His internal organs were fine. Peanut allergy was definitely the cause of death. Just one peanut can do it if the person has a severe allergy.'

'Were there bowls of peanuts around?'

'No. His wife had notices up in the kitchen that no meals or snacks should contain nuts. That wasn't just for his sake, but in case of litigation if one of the patients should be allergic to nuts.'

'So where did the nut come from?'

Lorna shrugged. 'Who knows? They tried to blame the chef who prepared the prunes and bacon.'

'Devils on horseback?'

'You've heard of them,' she said in surprise. 'Retro food of the sixties, I believe. There was a plate of them in the kitchen.'

'Why was he in the kitchen anyway?'

Lorna resumed eating. Suki had eaten very little of her fish pie, and my appetite for my roast chicken was fast disappearing. After a few moments, Lorna looked up miserably from her plate. 'To get more food, I suppose. That's why I was there. The chef had told us there was extra food in the kitchen. Some of it was in the fridge, but the prunes and bacon were on a table covered with cling film. At least, most of them were covered in cling film. Rupert had obviously pulled back the cling film and eaten one. A bit of the prune was found in his hand.'

'Had he been drinking?'

'Of course he had. We'd all been drinking.'

'Spirits? Wine?'

'Punch, mostly, with lots of fruit in it. It looked innocuous enough, but there was brandy in it.'

'Did you drink it, Suki?' Suki had only sipped at her wine, Lorna had downed at least three glasses and I was on my second.

'Yes. It had a nice taste.'

'Were you drunk?'

She smiled shyly. 'First time,' she said. 'I got very dizzy. Never again.'

A few minutes later, the arrival of the dessert menu stopped all conversation. Lorna had by now cleared her plate, but she chose sticky toffee pudding with cream. Suki and I chose ice cream, not because we really wanted it, but perhaps because we didn't want to appear too virtuous in the face of Lorna's obvious eating problem. Diets did work, I thought, but only for those who over-ate the wrong things or didn't move enough, but a diet can never help an emotional problem. Lorna didn't need a dietician or a surgeon, she needed a psychiatrist.

It was Suki who suggested we change the subject. 'Please, no more talk about death.'

Lorna, having finished her pudding, looked up. 'What else is there but death, illness, gossip and sex?' I might have suggested everything from astrophysics to Zen Buddhism, but I didn't want to sound like a smart-arse, so I said, 'Gossip sounds OK. Is there any?'

Lorna gave a little laugh. 'At Fair Acres we don't have MRSA. But we do have GRAS – short for galloping rumour and supposition.'

'What's the latest?'

'That Mark Alba is having an affair with Louise Booth.'

I thought of Louise in her smart suit and tried to imagine her with short, balding Mark. I couldn't.

'I got the impression,' I said, 'that he was gay.'

'That minor point doesn't stop the gossip mongers,' said Lorna, glancing at Suki's leftover ice cream.

'Who is the worst gossip in the place?'

'That's easy,' said Lorna. 'It's Alice. She's got something to say about everyone. And that bitch in the sewing room. It's a pity she doesn't drop down dead. She says she's anorexic, but if she *was*, she'd know what it's like to have an eating disorder.'

I sympathized. Doris's sharp words could make even a slimmish person feel elephantine.

'I've met Alice. I heard she'd had a tragic life.'

'If you ask me, the reason she hasn't been sacked by now is because she has a hold over someone.'

'What sort of hold?'

'The sort that comes from being a real snoop. She listens at keyholes, reads things she shouldn't and thinks she knows everything. She's not just a tragic victim ... she's dangerous...'

'I've worked with her,' interrupted Suki. 'She was fine to me.'

'Well, she would be,' snapped Lorna. 'You're a little workhorse. And she knows you're doing your best for your children. You don't know what she says about you behind your back though, do you?'

'No, and I don't want to,' answered Suki in a surprisingly sharp tone.

'Fair enough,' said Lorna. 'It'll be interesting to hear the gossip that starts about you, Kate. Already I've heard you were chatting Rav up. That won't get you very far. It's rumoured he's already having an affair.'

'I thought he was engaged.'

'He hoped that would stop the gossip.'

'So who is it?'

'Polly, the Aussie.'

'Really?' I asked in surprise. I tried hard to think back to our conversation. It was time, I thought, to start taking notes.

'Yep. It seems it started at the party.'

All roads, it seemed, led to the party. Our waitress appeared then, and we ordered coffee. Suki, by now, was looking tired and a bit fed up. I wanted to ask more questions, but I didn't want them to get suspicious of me.

When the coffee arrived, and Lorna had ladled sugar into her cup and stirred it at length, she said, 'There is one more rumour.'

Suki looked uncomfortable. 'You're the one starting that one,' she said. 'You're only guessing.'

'I should have been a detective,' said Lorna. She leant forward to tell me. 'I reckon Victoria Decker-White has a problem with the insurance company.'

'In what way?'

'He was worth a fortune, and word is he'd taken out a huge life insurance policy recently.'

'But if the police say his was an accidental death, surely that's the end of the matter.'

'It's not over till the fat lady sings,' she said with a wry smile.

81

'So you think the case isn't really closed?'
Lorna nodded.

'But Victoria seemed to be devastated by her husband's death. Surely you don't think she deliberately poisoned him?'

'I don't think he was an angel.'

'He is now,' said Suki sharply.

'You're not the police,' said Lorna, 'and they were satisfied it was an accident.' Suki glanced down at her wristwatch. 'I don't want to be back late, Lorna. I'm on early shift in the morning.'

Lorna sighed but used her mobile phone. 'We're in luck. Ten minutes.'

By the time we'd paid the bill and slipped on our jackets, the ten minutes was nearly up. I'd noticed Lorna paid for Suki's meal, and I guessed, by Suki's downcast expression, she would have rather spent the evening alone.

We stood outside, waiting for the taxi to appear. The night was clear and frost was beginning to appear. In a perverse sort of way, I'd enjoyed the evening. I wasn't sure I'd learned much, but enough to know that behind Fair Acres' respectable exterior lay intrigue and maybe murder.

On the way back, Lorna fell asleep. Suki whispered to me that she worried about her. We had to rouse her once we'd stopped, and she was barely awake as I paid the silent, elderly taxi driver, a man whose careworn expression said he'd seen it all, and whose eyes showed blank indifference even to my generous tip.

Suki took Lorna's arm. They made an incongruous sight walking together in front of me – the frail and beautiful and the big and ungainly.

The taxi had parked near my car, and I decided I'd lived quite long enough without the company of my TV, so I lugged it slowly up the stairs in the semi-dark. There was no sign of Lorna and Suki in the corridor, and I heard no voices. All was quiet.

Nine

The following morning, only half-awake, because I'd watched a late-night film on TV, I began writing a few notes. Mostly the names of staff who I knew had attended the New Year party. I guessed some of the guests would be relatives or friends of those on the staff. Top of my list, though, was an evening visit to Victoria. I lost track of time and was five minutes late for work. Mark looked daggers at me – after all, there was no excuse, as I did live on the premises. There was no sign of Alice at the handover from the night staff. Polly was the RN, and there were two other care assistants – Beryl and Julie. Julie, the younger one, was about thirty-five, but looked a little careworn; Beryl was older, well made-up, and into her fifties. As the night sister gave us the report in a sleepy monotone, Julie gave me a wink. It was only seven forty a.m., but already one patient was in theatre and another waiting to go. Polly was assigned to immediate post-op care, and we carers were assigned to beds, washes and bed baths.

The morning passed without any dramas, and I enjoyed working with Julie, who was efficient and calm. During our coffee break, she chatted about her four children, her difficult mother-in law and how awful the local schools were. It didn't need much response from me, and in fifteen minutes I barely spoke.

Mark sent us to first lunch at twelve fifteen, and as we stared at the rather mundane selection of food waiting to be served, Julie said, 'When Pat, the last cook, was here the food was great. She was always trying out new things.'

'What happened to her?' I asked.

'She was forced to resign. Over one single peanut she knew nothing about.'

'I heard about that. Stuffed in a prune, wasn't it?'

'Yeah, but why would Pat do that?'

'She wasn't suspected of doing it on purpose, was she?'

Julie was about to reply when the kitchen assistant said, 'What would you like, ladies?'

'I'll be good,' said Julie. 'A baked potato with tuna and salad, please.'

I chose the same and we sat down at an empty table for four. 'I'm watching my weight,' she said. 'My old man says having jollies with me is like climbing the Himalayas, because my belly is so big.'

'You look perfectly normal to me.'

'I wear pull-the-tum-in knickers. When I take them off, my belly cascades out.'

'I think you're exaggerating.'

'I'm bloody not. You haven't had any kids, have you?'

I agreed I hadn't. We ate in silence for a while until I said, 'What were you saying about the cook?'

'Oh yeah. Poor old Pat. The police really grilled her and she was a bit sensitive about it all and she decided to leave.'

'But if Pat didn't put the peanut in the prune, then who did?'

Julie shrugged. 'God knows. Rupert was a friendly easy-going type. Not stuck up like some of the surgeons who work here.'

'Was he a bit of a womanizer?'

'I never heard that he was. Although Victoria seemed to keep a close eye on him at the party.'

'So it was an accident?'

'I think so,' she said thoughtfully. 'Maybe wherever those prunes came from – that's where the peanut crept in. Once I found a rusty nail in a tin of beans. These things happen.'

I have to admit I hadn't thought of that possibility, but no doubt the police had. And more to the point, the chances of a peanut-allergy sufferer eating the one prune with a peanut in the middle must be millions to one.

Julie looked at her watch. I wanted to ask her more, but there was no time. We went back to the ward and I was given the job of looking after a vomiting patient. It was not the best afternoon of my life, but at least by the time I left, my patient had settled and told me I was an angel, so my afternoon did have its compensations.

Back in my room just after four, I rang Victoria. She sounded low in spirits, which wasn't surprising, but she suggested I came for supper about seven. Food and conversations over and about food seemed to be at the forefront of my undercover work. I didn't mind, but I could see why Doris complained about people getting fatter. Food is the ultimate comfort, although, remembering my afternoon's work, I wished I'd only agreed to coffee and a biscuit.

I showered and dressed and was about to ring Hubert when my mobile rang. It was David. 'Sorry about last time we spoke,' he said. 'I was just hacked off at having to go on yet another course.'

'How's it going?'

'Don't ask, Kate. I'll be back at the week-end. What about you?'

'I'm off Friday and Saturday.'

'What about a meal out Saturday night?'

'Sounds good,' I said, but what I really meant was: what about going ten-pin bowling, or dancing or going to the theatre or to a casino? But I didn't say anything, because Longborough didn't cater for those tastes, and David didn't have much imagination anyway.

'I'll pick you up at eight. How's Hubert?'

'Fine.' I paused. 'I take it you haven't heard?'

'Heard what?'

'He's getting married.'

'You're joking!'

'I'm not. He's met some American woman on the Internet and wedding bells are not far off. Providing, that is, they even like each other.'

'They haven't met?'

'Hubert would call it a meeting of minds – she's a much-married embalmer.'

'Silly old fool.'

'Exactly.'

'You're upset about it?'

'Upset?' I said. 'Of course I am. I don't want him to ruin his life.'

'What you mean is, you don't want life to change.'

'Maybe.'

'There's no maybe about it, Kate. You and Hubert are as cosy as one of those slippers where two feet go into one.'

'That sounds obscene.'

'It's the truth.'

I didn't respond. He was right, of course. We were far too cosy, and I didn't want my life to change.

'We'll talk about this Saturday night,' said David. 'How's the case going?'

'No problems,' I said.

'Well, if you do need help, I'll do my best.'

He was obviously feeling sorry for me, or he had other intentions. 'I can manage. So far I haven't cocked up.'

As I was about to hang up, he said, 'I've missed you.'

Had I missed him? I'd missed Jasper and Hubert, but in truth I hadn't given David a lot of thought. And, as I had a mission which involved driving to somewhere unfamiliar, I studied my AA map and hoped I'd find Upper Tapston in the dark with the minimum of aggravation.

I left Fair Acres at six thirty p.m. The night was dank and murky, with no sign of a moon. So far I'd only seen the area in the

89

dark, and I was surprised to find a small village with a pub and a shop about ten minutes' walk away. I soon found signs to Lower Tapston and eventually the road to Upper Tapston. Upper Tapston was a smaller village than Lower Tapston, and although it had a church with a fine steeple, the only shop was an antique shop. Thatched cottages, detached houses, a village pond and an air of money and quiet gentility pervaded the place. There was no sign of life and so no one to ask the way to Longmore Lane. I continued driving and, once through the heart of the village, which I thought was barely beating, I found the lane to my left. It was single-track and interminably long, although when a four-bar gate barred my way, with pine trees on the other side, I knew I'd arrived.

I was wearing jeans and trainers and tacky earth clung to the soles. Once past the gate and the pines, I seemed to be on solid ground, and now the house came into full view. It had the rambling exterior and outhouses that suggested it had once been a farmhouse. There was no sign of a car, but one of the outbuildings, possibly once a cowshed, had an up-and-over garage door, and looked big enough to house two or three cars.

Lights were on downstairs, and as I approached the front door, a security light flashed on. The door was red, with a knocker and a bell. I knocked first and waited. Then I pushed the button and in the silence could hear it trilling around the house. I waited for what seemed ages, then made my way round to the back of the building. At the back, I was surprised to find a large covered patio area and a swimming pool covered by blue tarpaulin. Peering through a back window to the kitchen, the inside was a surprise. This was no cosy farmhouse with an Aga and a Welsh dresser. Victoria's kitchen was all chrome and steel, with black and white accessories. More to the point, there was no response from my knocking on the back door. I glanced at my watch. It was five minutes to seven. I doubted if she'd popped out for a pint of milk, so I tried the handle of the back door. It was open.

Gingerly, I made my way inside, trying to disregard all the films I'd seen where somewhere in the house lies a body. I called her name and moved swiftly from the kitchen to the other ground-floor rooms. The style was minimalist and as impersonal as a show house. Mostly black and white, the sitting room gave the impression that high-flying thirty-somethings had bought the place on some buy-to-let scheme and had misjudged the market.

I called out several times, and as I began walking upstairs, although the stair carpet was plush, the floorboards creaked. Trepidation had now taken hold. In the kitchen, there had been no smell nor sign of any supper. Apart from the sounds I was making, there were no others. On the landing, the bathroom door was open and traces of steam and sweet-smelling soap still lingered. The shower was separate from the bath, and the door slightly open and misted. I didn't look too closely. In the master bedroom, white bed linen and peach walls gave the room a feminine look. There were two more bedrooms in pastel colours, and a room with a locked door. Where the hell was Victoria? Unless, of course, she was behind the locked door.

My imagination didn't run riot any further, because I heard the sound of a car drawing up. I raced downstairs and out of the kitchen. I heard the car door slam and I waited a few seconds before knocking on the back door.

When Victoria let me in, she said, 'It was open. Have you been waiting long?'

'I'd just arrived,' I said. She wore a black low-necked dress and high heels, as if she'd just returned from a cocktail party. Her mascara had run a little, her face was flushed and her eyes were bright, but I told myself not to jump to any conclusions.

'You've caught me out, I'm afraid,' she said, sounding fairly cheerful. 'I was planning to convince you I'd cooked a meal, but a kind neighbour has cooked for us. It just needs warming up in the microwave.'

From a carrier bag, she produced two plated meals. 'Casseroled pheasant,' she informed me. 'But let's have a drink first.'

In the sitting room, she switched on an ultra-modern gas fire and an uplighter lamp, the light of both making the room slightly more cosy. 'Sit down and make yourself comfortable. If you can in this hideous place. Not my choice, I can assure you. It reminds me of a Manhattan lawyer's office – cold and businesslike.'

I could neither agree nor disagree, never having seen the inside of one, so I murmured something about it being very fashionable.

'Rupert thought it would make him feel younger. He was terrified of growing old ... ironic, isn't it?'

I nodded.

'White or red wine?' she asked.

'Either,' I said, 'but only one small glass.'

'You can always stay the night,' she said,

smiling.

As she left the room to fetch the wine, I thought if she proved talkative I might well stay the night. And for someone off sick with the stress of bereavement, she seemed to me to be remarkably cheerful.

Normally in a room there are photos and knick-knacks to look at. Here there was a clock, a few geometric prints and one vase of red roses. On the glass coffee table rimmed in chrome sat a bowl of less than fresh fruit.

Victoria brought in two opened bottles of wine and two large glasses on a tray. I chose red and realized from the size of the glass I *would* be staying the night. It soon became obvious when Victoria downed her glass almost in one that she had a problem.

'Sorry to be such a pig. I'm in a state really. Everyone thinks I'm holding up well. But I'm being propped up by alcohol – as you can see.'

She drank the second glass more slowly. I merely sipped mine. I had a feeling the pheasant casserole was some way off.

'Have you found out anything?' she asked as she kicked off her high heels.

I sat back on the upright sofa that offered no head or bum comfort and gave her a weak but true answer. 'I've obviously had a few casual conversations. Your husband was very popular and so far I've found no motive for anyone to want to harm him.'

'Yes, he was very popular,' she agreed. 'I've never been popular there, I suppose I'm always talking cutbacks and economies and I rarely leave my office. Until now, that is. I'm not planning to go back.'

I was surprised. 'Should you make an important decision like that quite so soon?'

'It was Rupert's presence there that made it bearable,' she said draining her glass. 'Now he's gone there is really no need for me to stay.'

'What makes you dislike Fair Acres so much?'

She flashed me an inquiring glance as if asking how I could be quite so stupid. She poured herself another glass of wine and topped mine up. 'Some women see surgeons like wild game ... to be hunted. Married or single it makes no difference. In fact some women prefer married men. It means they get the thrill of the chase and the feeling of superiority when they make their final kill.'

'Are you saying you think a woman murdered your husband?' I asked. 'Just because he rejected her advances?'

'You're the detective,' she said with a slight sneer.

On an empty stomach I felt the wine going

to my head and already my senses seemed slightly dulled. Victoria, in contrast, appeared sharp and edgy. Killing by a peanut stuffed into a prune did seem an unlikely method for a man but I didn't want to jump to any conclusions. The image that did spring to mind was Eve offering Adam an apple. If there was a murder it was done that way – proffering the poisoned devil on horseback, even putting it into his mouth. Who would do that but someone who knew Rupert very well indeed? Someone who proffered him something most days. A scrub nurse. The theatre sister?

I was working in the wrong place.

Ten

'Tell me about the theatre staff,' I said.

Victoria looked pensive. 'I know he regarded the theatre manager Lynsey Page very highly.'

'What's she like?' I asked.

'Married with two children. Fairly ordinary looking. In her forties.'

'Did you ever suspect there was anything going on between them?'

Victoria laughed derisively. 'No, of course not.'

'How can you be so sure?' She hesitated and for a moment I thought she was going to say again that Rupert was interested in other women.

'Rupert looked for women who could offer him something.'

'You mean money?'

She nodded. 'Money, property, fast cars. He would not have married me if I'd been poor. He was planning early retirement ... you know the sort of thing ... a yacht, a property abroad – a life of leisure.'

'You sound as if that doesn't appeal to you.'

'It doesn't. I'd be bored rigid. I hate the sea and boats.'

'So was that a cause of friction?'

'No because Rupert was a control freak and for a quiet life I kept my mouth shut and just hoped his retirement wouldn't happen for a long time.'

She stared at me for a moment as if realizing that the idyllic marriage she'd described before was getting a little tarnished. 'I think we should eat now, don't you? Dining room or kitchen?'

'Kitchen's fine by me.'

We sat amongst the steel and chrome on high-back chairs at the breakfast bar to eat. The pheasant was pleasant but Victoria, like royalty, pushed her food around the plate.

'Your neighbour's a good cook,' I said.

'Yes he is,' she answered staring at her plate and offering nothing further on the subject. I didn't ask but I knew her flushed face and bright eyes hadn't been caused by the sight of a pheasant casserole.

'Do they live near by?' I asked, thinking that a fairly innocuous question.

'Yes. I could walk there but I don't.'

Dessert was a brandy. Victoria was soon on her second and the alcohol had begun to take effect. Her words were slurring slightly and when she stood up for us to go back to the sitting room she swayed. It was possible she'd also been drinking with her neighbour and I took advantage of her condition by asking her about the night Rupert died. She wasn't *that* drunk because she ignored my question to say, 'The police and the insurance company suspect me.'

'Why's that?'

'I'm chief ... bene–ficiary. One million pounds will ... come my way eventually. So I'll be a rich widow, won't I?'

'What will you do with the money?'

She laughed. 'Have a damn good time.' She slumped back in the white leather chair, her head lolling slowly forwards.

'It's not late, try to stay awake,' I urged. Some people become more talkative with alcohol, others quieter. She was obviously in the latter group and if she fell asleep I would be wasting my time. 'I'm not asleep, I'm just resting my eyes,' she drawled.

'Tell me about the night of the party,' I said. 'Who decided the menu?'

'The person who paid for it.'

'Who was that?'

'Rupert, of course.'

'And the booze?'

'Oh ... yes. Rupert liked good wine...' She broke off.

'And women?' I queried.

'He liked a pretty face...'

Silence. Her head was slumped. But I was unwilling to give up just yet.

'Why did he go into the kitchen, Victoria?' I asked loudly. 'Where were you at the time?'

'I don't bloody know. Don't keep shouting at me ... let me sleep. It wasn't my fault.'

'What wasn't your fault?'

'Go away. Leave me alone.'

'I'll let you sleep for a while,' I said.

I put the television on with the sound down and closed my eyes. I woke up some time later to find Victoria standing over me. 'I'm making coffee,' she said. 'Want some?' My mouth felt full of sawdust and I only managed a nod. She left the room and I closed my eyes again.

When she reappeared with mugs of coffee she looked surprisingly awake and cheerful. Call me stupid but it took ages for me to recognize the obvious. An elephant with a millstone round its neck would have realized quicker than I did. I took a close look at the pupils of her eyes and finally asked her, 'What have you just taken?'

'Nothing,' she snapped. 'You're being paid by me to investigate Rupert's death so why don't you do just that.'

Victoria sat down with coffee and began

watching television. I sipped mine in silence. After a while the silence grew uncomfortable. 'If you don't want to cooperate with me,' I said, 'perhaps I should abandon the case.'

'Don't say that, Kate. Of course I want you to continue. I'm not a druggie but I do binge drink occasionally. The insurance company is giving me a hard time and although the police say they have closed the case...' She broke off. 'I'm not thinking too clearly. But I do know the person who killed Rupert shouldn't get away with it.'

'I agree but I do need your help,' I replied. 'And I get the feeling you're not being entirely honest with me.'

'I can't talk any more now,' she said. 'I just want to sleep and I'm sure you're tired too. Come again next week, you may have more information by then.'

Later in the guest room I lay awake wishing she'd sacked me. Apart from finding out the source of the prunes and speaking to Pat the ex-chef I didn't have much idea of what to do next. Gossip and innuendo was all very well but I needed some hard facts. Had the police found the same thing? With no forensic clues or indeed motive, what hope did they have? One phrase of Victoria's did reverberate – 'It wasn't my fault.'

In the morning I washed and dressed quickly and crept out hoping I hadn't woken Victoria. It was still dark, the air felt dank and cold and I wished I'd stayed long enough for breakfast.

The roads were empty and I arrived at Fair Acres with twenty-five minutes to spare. In the kitchen on the top floor I made tea and toast and stood eating it and staring out of the window. Lorna lumbering in broke my reverie. 'Where were you last night?' she said as she filled a tumbler with milk.

'Just visiting a friend and as I'd had a drink I couldn't drive home.'

'I didn't know you had a friend round here,' said Lorna, sounding somewhat suspicious.

'I hadn't seen her in years,' I said, 'so thought I'd make the effort.'

Lorna drank her milk so fast that rivulets ran down her chin. She wiped herself with the back of her hand and with a 'See ya', she left the kitchen.

On Washington ward the handover of the night staff was punctuated by moans and complaints. The kitchen had been untidy, flowers not put in water, a patient's supper forgotten – the complaints seemed endless and the young staff nurse looked near to tears. Mark ushered us away with a list of

102

tasks and room numbers that the three of us carers were to be responsible for. He led the night staff nurse, who by now was in tears, towards the patients' dayroom. I got the impression there was something more seriously amiss than a mere untidy kitchen.

Polly had a day off and I was working with Beryl and Julie. 'I've got that old moaner in room nine,' said Beryl. 'I bet it was his supper that didn't appear.' They both laughed and ignored me. I was still an outsider, an unknown quantity. I checked the list and began my shift.

The morning flashed by, and still Beryl and Julie seemed to be keeping me at arm's length. Mark caught up with me as I left a patient's room at midday, and asked me to check the drugs with him. For DDAs, which includes drugs such as pethidine and diamorphine, two RNs are required to check each item and to attend the patient together. Ordinary medicines just require two members of staff, only one of whom needs to be trained. Certain drugs, not just DDAs, are kept in locked cupboards, and only the RN in charge carries the keys. Mark, unusually, wanted me to check the ward stock of temazepam sleeping tablets. 'I've checked them once today,' he said, 'and the zopliclone. The night staff has found a discrepancy, so I'm checking them three times a day from now on.' He shook the tablets into a triangular counter. There were ten missing.

'Ten,' he muttered. 'I can cope with the odd one or two, but this is serious. Someone is nicking them, but I don't know who.'

'For their own use, or to sell?'

'I don't know. When the temazepam was in liquid form, addicts would syringe out the contents of the capsule and inject it. Now they probably crush them and mix them with water, and in no time at all they have veins like gravel pits.'

'Have you reported it to Louise?'

He looked at me sharply. 'Not yet. She'll call the police in and there'll be all sorts of problems. I'll sort it myself. We'll just have to be extra vigilant. And I don't want you talking about this – do you understand?'

I nodded. I got the impression this had happened before. Because only trained staff held the keys, it was the RNs who were under suspicion. Agency staff were often suspect, but Fair Acres rarely used them. The missing tablets were another mystery, I thought, that seemed unsolvable. At this rate I had visions of myself attending next year's New Year party.

At one p.m. a staff nurse appeared, to relieve Mark for lunch. He ushered me out of the ward, saying, 'I've had it up to here,' as he flicked his hand against his chin. The cafeteria was busy and we joined a table for four, to sit next to the handsome anaesthetist and a rather glamorous care assistant. It was then I saw a different side to Mark – flirtatious and touchy-feely. The care assistant, Sophie Rails, was young and blonde, had blue eyes, an angelic face and a mouth like a sewer. But it wasn't her Mark was interested in, it was Rav. No wonder he'd had to invent an imaginary fiancée. Sophie was a dab hand at obscene gestures, and when Mark spoke she made it clear what she thought he was. Mark, thankfully, didn't notice, but it was hard to keep a straight face.

On the way back to the ward, Mark said, 'I can't help it. I'm in love with the guy.'

'He is very attractive.'

'You think so too?' he said, as if surprised.

I wondered if he'd heard the rumour about Polly and Rav. He couldn't have failed to hear most rumours, because they seemed to spread as fast as water from a broken dam. I wasn't going to mention it, but as if reading my mind, he said, 'I know I've got no chance, but I can dream.'

Back on the ward, two men in grey suits stood by the nurse's station. I guessed they were police.

Eleven

The two men remained a mystery, and although I'd been vigilant, even trying to listen at keyholes, by late Friday afternoon I was still no wiser. I'd even said casually to Mark, 'They look like cops,' but he hadn't responded. Nothing, though, could diminish my joy at my first week being over. I finished at four p.m., my bag was packed and I was really looking forward to seeing Jasper and Hubert again. Although I'd spoken on the phone to Hubert, it just wasn't the same, and I longed to sleep in my own bed, have a proper conversation with him, and a home-cooked meal.

It was only as I was getting changed that I noticed the weather. It was snowing. Big flakes that were likely to settle. I'd hardly noticed the weather all week, because Fair Acres was no different to any other hospital temperature-wise – a tad above tropical. The snow made me hurry, although nothing short of a major blizzard would have stopped me starting out.

I drove carefully but thankfully, although it was slow going, the traffic kept moving and I approached Longborough at a respectable six forty-five p.m. Hubert stood in the doorway with Jasper wriggling in his arms. After much petting and tail wagging and licking my face, Jasper quietened and Hubert and I hugged a little self-consciously.

The kitchen table looked quite splendid with its white cloth and red paper napkins left over from Christmas. Hubert had wine and glasses at the ready and, with Jasper on my lap, I began to feel a real surge of happiness. I felt even happier after the first glass of wine, but at the first mention of Shirley-Marie, my spirits plummeted. He was as besotted as ever. 'She could be here within four weeks,' he said excitedly. Ask me about *me*, I thought selfishly. 'She really is a soulmate,' he said.

'Not allergic to peanuts, is she?' I asked.

'Naughty, naughty,' tutted Hubert. 'I know you don't mean it.'

I bloody *did*. My thoughts on Shirley-Marie were at that moment entirely murderous.

Hubert opened the oven and began basting the beef and turning the roast potatoes, but finally he sat down beside me. 'Now then, how have you been faring in the undercover world of lies and deceit?'

'How did you know?'

'I've watched plenty of hospital dramas.'

'This is real life, I suppose, and it's a bit murky and people aren't quite what they seem.'

'You're a case in point, aren't you?' said Hubert, sipping his wine. 'You're not what you seem. Beneath that nurse's uniform beats a snooper's heart.'

'I've missed you, Hubert, but sometimes I do wonder why.'

'Carry on telling me what you found out, and I'll just take the beef out and let it rest.'

'You've been watching the cookery programmes.'

'My mother,' said Hubert as he removed the beef, 'used to spend all of Sunday morning roasting a mean little joint until it was tough enough to sole a shoe with, and then the next day we had to endure it again cold. Those were the good old days.'

'Sounds like child abuse to me. Although cooking anything was beyond the scope of my mother.'

Hubert sat down. 'Spill the beans – or should it be peanuts?'

Sometimes Hubert's 'jokes' are extremely childish, so I smiled to humour him.

'I haven't found much out, except that, on the night of the party, most people were pretty well oiled. And I have a suspicion that there may be a bit of a drug culture going on.'

'And that's it?'

'Don't sound so surprised. I have to be very careful. I told you I was seeing Victoria. She's drinking heavily, and I think she may have snorted coke while I was with her. She can't be the only one, can she?'

'Supplier on the premises, do you think?' asked Hubert as he tested the vegetables with a fork.

'I don't know for sure, but it seems likely.'

'What about motive? Are you thinking money or lust and jealousy?'

'All three are a real possibility, but we're talking very tangled webs.'

'What about the photos that were taken at the party, do they help?'

My mouth dropped. 'What do you mean, Hubert – what photos?'

'Someone always has a camera at a do, or even a camcorder.'

'You're a genius,' I said, jumping up to kiss his forehead, but after the euphoria came the realization that I should have thought of it first. And guessing there were photos didn't mean I could get hold of them.

The well-rested beef and all the accompaniments were absolutely delicious. Jasper, as usual at mealtimes, sat quietly under the table, patient, waiting. Hubert tried to hide the fact that he was feeding Jasper the choicest titbits of beef under the table. I was doing the same thing, but we both acted surreptitiously, as if we were sneak thieves and not just sneaky feeders.

It was dessert that came as a shock. 'Is this your idea of a joke?' I said, staring into a plate of prunes and custard.

'No,' he said, 'it's in the name of research I've been doing on your behalf. I bought a vacuum pack of the best prunes from Chile, and rang the company in the UK that distributes them...'

'I had thought of that,' I said, interrupting his flow. 'I just haven't had a chance to do it.'

'Listen up,' he said. 'I told their PR director I'd heard one of their prunes contained a peanut. She didn't seem that surprised. The company cover themselves from litigation by printing a warning on the packet, stating that it may contain nuts. It's obvious that they can't open every single prune, and although cases have been rare, a foreign body does slip in occasionally on the Chilean side of the operation.'

'So you think I'm chasing a fluke – an

accident?'

'Sure do!'

'Stop talking like a pseudo-American. We'll have enough of that when the real thing arrives.'

'Eat your prunes, they're good for you.'

I ate them, dissecting each one first. They were all perfect.

'What if I told you,' I said, 'that Victoria stood to gain a million pounds plus from her husband's estate, and I think she's having an affair with a neighbour?'

Hubert looked thoughtful. 'I'd say she could have committed the perfect murder, and if she's a junkie, she'll need plenty of money to feed her habit.'

'Not likely, though, that she'd employ a PI, is it?'

'Could be a clever ploy,' said Hubert, collecting up the plates and gesturing with his hand that hc didn't need my help. 'She may be arrogant enough to think it will strengthen her case when she tells the police your findings.'

'So, you're assuming I won't find her guilty?'

'I've every confidence in you, but don't be disappointed if you come to the same con-clusion as the police.'

'I don't think the police have given up on

111

the case. Two men, dead ringers for cops, were on the ward today.'

Hubert made coffee and we retired to the lounge, where we slumped for a while in silence. Eventually Hubert said, 'I looked up Decker-White on the Internet.'

'And?'

'It seems he worked as a gynaecologist in this country, but in Canada he worked in a small private hospital as a general surgeon.'

'That's it? No scandal? No botched jobs?'

'Give me a chance. There was a mention that he worked for three years in the North-Western Territory, in a remote township called Eagle Ridge.'

'What happened?'

'I had to spend hours on the World Wide Web to find out, but I managed to talk via the Internet to the owner of a local newspaper, and it seems there was a botched op or two. One woman haemorrhaged to death and another was left disabled by some sort of repair job.'

'Why wasn't he struck off?'

'I think the attitude was he was working alone and doing his best. But ... there was a suggestion he was drinking heavily, so he made a hasty exit and began working in a hospital near Toronto.'

'No scandals there?'

'It seems he redeemed himself. At least, I couldn't find anything.'

'I think you should be the detective,' I said.

'It beats undertaking. I could always sell up.'

'Don't get any ideas, sweetheart,' I said firmly. 'Remember your intended. And when she comes over, you won't have to pay for the locum embalmer.'

'You've never called me sweetheart before. I must be in your good books.'

'You are, Hubert. You are.'

Much as I appreciated Hubert's efforts, two botched ops in Canada approximately ten years back, and the fact that the peanut may have been a pure accident, didn't really help me much.

Just as I began to think about going to bed, Hubert said, 'There is something else. Rupert was very fond of holidaying in Thailand, and for the last three years he's gone there with Victoria on a recruiting drive.'

Hubert went to bed, followed closely by Jasper, and I sat up thinking. What surprised me was that Louise Booth, being director of nursing, hadn't been the one to do the recruiting. Thailand was another angle, but did it have any significance? All roads led back to Victoria, it seemed. And why hadn't Suki volunteered the information that the

113

Decker-Whites had recruited her?

Past midnight, I told myself I'd sleep on it, and although I did sleep, I had recurring nightmares about car accidents.

Over breakfast, I mentioned it to Hubert. 'Didn't you say there'd been a hit and run accident and a member of staff was killed?' he asked. Not only had I forgotten about the accident, I'd forgotten her name. I dredged through my memory banks, but it was only when I stopped trying to remember that it came to me – Trina Brampton.

'I've remembered,' I told Hubert. 'Maybe that's something I could follow up as a bona fide PI.'

'I'd be careful,' said Hubert, frowning. 'She was bound to have friends at the hospital. Word will soon get round.'

'You're right,' I said. 'But I could find out more from the boy who was driving.'

'He could be a right tearaway,' warned Hubert. 'Just watch your back, and in future take jobs close to home. *Comprende?*'

I smiled. *'Si, si, Señor.'*

The spectre of Shirley-Marie rose again. She was even changing his vocabulary.

Hubert had a call-out shortly afterwards, giving me the opportunity to ring Victoria.

'I'm sorry about last night,' she said. 'I've been somewhat out of control since Rupert died.'

'I understand. It wasn't a problem and I enjoyed my meal and the wine. The reason I've rung is that I need access to staff files. Would that be possible?'

There was a long pause before she said, 'I do have keys and access to everywhere. I am a major shareholder – *the* major shareholder since Rupert died.'

'Who are the other shareholders?' I asked.

'I'll give you a list when I see you, but none of them has a major financial interest in the hospital.'

'When you said you'd leave your job, does that include selling your shares in Fair Acres?'

'I haven't decided that yet,' she said sharply. 'Who are you interested in, in particular?'

'Trina Brampton.'

'Why?'

'Because her death was supposedly accidental...'

'Surely you don't think an uninsured teenager with no driving licence *deliberately* ran her down – that it was murder?'

'Doris seemed to think—' I began.

'That little scandal monger. She ought to be sacked. I'm sure she didn't tell you the full story. The investigation into Trina's death was very thorough, very thorough

115

indeed. It had to be.'

'Why?'

'Didn't Doris tell you?'

'Tell me what?'

'Trina was married to Police Superintendent Brian Brampton.'

It took me a few moments to ask the question. 'He wasn't, by any chance, at the New Year party, was he?'

Twelve

'Yes, Brian Brampton was there. Much to the disgust of many. Trina had only been dead for less than two months, and he swaggered in and flirted with any available woman.'

'No one mentioned him,' I said.

'They wouldn't. It's thought he has his little spy cell within the hospital.'

'He's the sort who would shop his own mother?'

Victoria sighed. 'He'd *sell* his own mother. I think he's dangerous, so be careful.'

'Thanks for the warning.'

'And don't get caught in Louise's office. There is a night-time security man, so make sure he's in another part of the building.'

'One other question,' I said. 'Do you know the name and address of the boy who ran down Trina?'

She paused for a moment. 'I think his first name was Brett or Brent but that's all I know. Someone who *will* know is Doris.

She'll probably have a copy of the local paper. I've heard she's a bit of a hoarder.'

'That'll save some time if she agrees to help me.'

'She'll be delighted, only she'll try not to show it.'

I was about to end the conversation when I remembered to ask about cameras.

'We didn't have one,' she said, 'but there were people using camera phones.'

My own mobile phone was practically an antique, so the idea of camera phones hadn't crossed my mind.

I thanked Victoria, and as I put down the phone, I felt a real surge of optimism that if I asked the right questions then the answers couldn't be far behind.

A long, cold walk with Jasper would be good for me, I decided, and as I slipped his lead on he managed a stretch and mini wag of his tail. For once I was keener than him. I'd missed our walks, and after the hot stuffy atmosphere of Fair Acres, a real blast of fresh air would be wonderful. I was about to leave when the phone rang. I hesitated. Jasper sat down and I let go of the lead and picked up the phone.

'Hi there. Is that Kate? This is Shirley-Marie. Howya doing? I've heard so much about you. Hubert thinks you're a real gem.'

'Does he?' I said.

'He sure does. I'm so looking forward to meeting you. We'll have a great time.'

'Doing what exactly?'

'You know, girly things – shopping and getting our nails done and having a massage.'

You'll be lucky, I thought, Longborough was somewhat short on hedonism. She was in for a shock.

'Anyway, Kate – is Hube there?'

'He's working.'

'Oh, what a shame. You be sure to tell him I called to send him my love and let him know I'll be over in two weeks' time. I'll ring him to let him know the flight details. I'm just so excited, and I can't wait to show you my dress. It's so pretty. You'll be green with envy.'

'Is it white and flouncy?' I asked.

She was impervious to the tone of my voice and my sarcasm. 'Yeah. White as snow, with big sleeves and a real full skirt.'

'I can't wait. I'll tell Hubert you called.'

'Great to speak to you, Kate. God bless and keep you,' she shouted enthusiastically.

My heart sank. She could well be an evangelical Christian. Any religion is fine as long as no one wants to convert me. Hubert held no religious convictions, so how come they were soulmates?

On the walk with Jasper, I tried not to think about Shirley-Marie, but her voice kept drifting into my mind. She was thick-skinned, that was for sure, but I wasn't – and I wasn't prepared to live with two people. I could, of course, stay at Fair Acres and try to avoid breaking my cover. I could even pro-long the investigation. Who was I kidding? It would take as long as it would take, and even then I might not discover the whole truth. And what was the truth? A wild party, a prune from Chile containing a peanut, and the one man with a nut allergy at that party eats it. His death was just a freak accident, like being hit by lightning, or my erstwhile boyfriend being killed by a falling brick. Trina Brampton's death also appeared to be accidental, hit by a joyrider who didn't stop – a tragedy that happens far too frequently. Even so, both so-called accidental deaths had enough elements of mystery to make me want to go on until the milk curdled. Talk of milk curdling was a favourite of a batty old woman I once nursed. No matter what the event, she'd shout, 'We'll go on till the milk curdles!' Now, with the imminent arrival of the God-fearing Ms Baker, I had a good enough reason to take my time and try to do my best investigation ever. And the milk could turn to cheese for all I cared.

Hubert came back mid-afternoon looking glum. If he didn't want to talk about a particular death, I didn't press him, but when I gave him Shirley-Marie's message, he broke into a smile. I hastily put the kettle on and began toasting crumpets just to keep myself busy.

'I'll give her a ring now,' he said as I placed his tea in front of him. I watched him leave the room and I felt a childish anger and disappointment that he preferred talking to her to my tea and crumpets. I went to my office, switched on my computer and began writing up my investigation so far. And I made a list of people to visit. I only hoped I'd have the energy after a day's work.

It took Hubert more than an hour to appear at my door. He thrust a mug of tea at me and asked what time I was going out. I told him eight.

'You two have a drink with me before you go,' he said. 'I really like David.'

As he walked away, he murmured, 'I do get lonely.'

I felt at that moment a real pang of guilt at being such a jealous bitch. Maybe he thought Shirley-Marie was, at his age, his last chance. And I was being a complete pain. I resolved there and then to be happy for Hubert and to be as pleasant as possible to his fiancée. My only proviso being I would be neither bridesmaid nor maid of honour.

David arrived on time and Hubert monopolized him in his office for half an hour with a computer problem. On their return, it was drinks all round, with Hubert insisting we took a taxi. There was a light covering of snow outside, and as we stood at my doorway waiting for the taxi to arrive, gentle flakes of snow began to fall, lending the car park a more romantic flavour. When the taxi eventually arrived, the romance continued, and I realized David had drunk more than I thought. He kept saying how much he'd missed me, and he wanted to have a serious talk about our future.

He'd chosen the same Italian restaurant that Hubert had taken me to the night he revealed his wedding plans. The same waiter with the pert bum whispered something to me in Italian as I sat down. I had a feeling he was calling me a tart.

The good food and wine began to mellow my mood. David was attentive and listened to my Fair Acres saga with real interest. But when he offered to help, I told him I was managing just fine.

'The day of the lone PI has long gone, Kate. Given half a chance, Hubert would give up his business, or at least have it managed and work alongside you.'

'He'd just try to take over and I'd slip into odd-job girl role.'

'I can't see you doing that,' he said with a smile. 'But you do tend to use Hubert like a security blanket. What if his fiancée wants him to go back to the USA with her?'

'He wouldn't go. I know he wouldn't.' My mellow mood was fast vanishing now, and David wasn't going to let the matter drop.

'That's not what he told me. He said if Shirley was unhappy, he'd follow her to the ends of the earth.'

'Yuk!'

'Don't be bitchy. Men in love tend to make extravagant gestures. I know you're undecided about getting married, but...'

'But what?'

'We could live together for a trial period. Especially if you and Shirley-Marie don't get on.'

I paused in surprise. 'It's a kind offer,' I murmured. 'And I will think about it, but until this case is sorted, I want to stay focused.'

David looked crestfallen but he rallied over dessert. 'I'm not giving up on you. Perhaps I haven't been attentive enough. Next week I'll be coming to Fair Acres and we'll go out somewhere.'

'Next week! I'll be far too busy.'

'Don't argue,' he said sharply. 'I'll be there.'

The following day, Sunday, I left Humberstone's at ten a.m. Jasper's tail was hanging low and Hubert looked correspondingly glum. I merely felt confused. David's attentions were beginning to make an impression, and for all my protestations of wanting to see the case through on my own, I did doubt my ability to do so. When he'd asked if I'd searched through Rupert's belongings, I had to admit I hadn't given it a thought. I'd been too busy eating and drinking wine with Victoria. I didn't even know if the police had searched the house, and somehow I doubted that they had.

Arriving back in my room at Fair Acres at twelve noon, I found a note under my door. I was to report at one p.m. to Churchill Ward. I guessed someone was off sick, and I didn't mind changing wards – new people, new perspective, I thought.

I'd changed into my uniform and was making tea in the kitchen when Lorna came in. The kitchen suddenly seemed a small place. 'I thought I heard you come in,' she said. 'Good time off?'

'Great, thanks.'

'You're lucky to have somewhere to go. Usually I just hang round here for my days off.'

'Don't you go anywhere with Suki?'

'She doesn't take much time off. The odd half day, but she needs all the money that she can earn.'

'I thought that was illegal,' I said. 'Working more than a certain number of hours.'

She laughed. 'Here? Don't be silly. Things are never quite what they seem, are they?'

'What do you mean?'

'You'll find out.'

She gave me a weird, knowing smile and left the kitchen.

At one o'clock, myself, one RN and one carer were given the morning report. Marie O'Grady the manager sent the others off to various duties and asked me to stay behind. 'I want you to help me with some paperwork,' she said. It was a perfectly ordinary statement and yet she looked pale and sounded anxious. 'I've got to order stationery and get the care plans in order and reorder from pharmacy. It's a lot to do.'

My heart sank, paperwork was not my favourite occupation, but it had to be done and Marie didn't seem able to cope on her own. She seemed twitchy and nervous, but perhaps that was her normal state. I did wonder why she'd picked me to help her, but as I tidied and counted various forms in the stationery cupboard, Marie completed and signed the order forms.

As the afternoon progressed, Marie seemed at times to lose concentration and she disappeared to the staff toilet every half hour or so. After her fourth visit, I asked if she was OK.

'I'm menopausal,' she said. 'My doctor thinks I need Prozac. I've been like this ever since my sister died. We shared a house. I want to move but I haven't got the energy. I don't sleep at night. I'm frightened of every noise. I'm even frightened of the dark.'

'How long is it since she died?' I asked.

'Four years.'

I was surprised at the length of time, but living alone, I knew, could affect some people badly. 'Have you any other family?'

'There's no one. We were left some money by an aunt and so we travelled all over.'

'Where did you go?'

'Australia, New Zealand, India, Thailand, the USA and Canada. We had a wonderful time.'

Thirteen

I tried not to look too interested or surprised, so I murmured something about always wanting to see the Rockies.

'Canada's a wonderful country,' said Marie, staring into the distance.

We were interrupted then by one of the carers, who'd been sent by the RN, who was worried about a new admission.

'Stay put,' said Marie as she rushed away. 'I'll be back. Start on the care plans.'

I was about to start when two new admissions arrived, an elderly man walking with a stick, the other a worried-looking middle-aged woman accompanied by a younger man. Trying to look as if I knew what I was doing, I found the necessary paperwork and directed them to the patients' lounge. When Marie came back, she looked harassed. 'Forget the care plans. You do the admissions. Have they arrived?'

'There are two in the lounge.'

'Rooms one and two for them. Make sure

your writing is legible.'

From then on, the afternoon descended into chaos. Surgeons and anaesthetists I'd never seen before arrived to examine patients pre-op. Two patients spiked temperatures and another complained of chest pain. I felt glad I didn't have any real responsibility, and by the time I left at nine, my blood sugar was low, having missed supper, and my adrenaline was high. I felt jumpy and anxious.

In my room, I paced around for a while, then decided to have a bath. Hunter-gathering would have to come later. As I lay in the bath, I summed up the day. All I'd learnt was that Marie O'Grady had once been to Canada. That could hardly be called a connection with Decker-White, Canada was a huge country and the chances of their meeting seemed remote. After my bath, I went to the kitchen, made tea and toast and, feeling better and more lively, decided I'd ring Victoria and ask if I could collect the master key. Sunday night might be fairly quiet, I thought.

I telephoned Victoria, apologized for it being late, and asked if I could come and collect the keys.

'How long will you be?'

'I'll be there in half an hour.'

Her reply sounded muffled and I had the impression that there was someone with her.

When I did arrive, a black or navy car was driving away fast, too fast for me to see the full number plate. I only managed the letters ORR. Victoria stood at the front door.

'Come on in. I need a drink,' were her first words. She looked pale and she'd been crying. She poured herself a large brandy and offered me one, which I refused. She drank quickly and took some deep breaths. 'I can't believe it,' she said. 'How could it happen?'

'Sit down and tell me about it,' I suggested, but instead she poured herself another brandy and ignored me. Then, as if remembering I was there, she offered me orange juice.

Finally she slumped down on the sofa. 'Talk to me,' I said. 'Who was your visitor?'

She looked at me sharply. 'She was a ghost, but you saw her, didn't you? So, she must have been real. How could he? I trusted him. I loved him. The bastard!'

'Who was she?' I asked quietly. She was getting hysterical and I didn't want to spend another night with her, so I knew I had to be patient and try to keep her calm.

'My visitor was a dead woman. Dead for

years, according to the snake I was married to.'

'Explain it to me.'

'I don't understand myself. I wish I did...' She broke off to take a huge gulp of brandy. 'That woman was Mrs Decker-White. In law, she's his legal wife. He wasn't a widower when I married him. Worse than that, he's been sending her money for years – our money. She's come over here to find out why the payments have stopped. What the hell am I going to do?'

I kept quiet. What could I say? She rambled on, sometimes incoherently, then she sobbed and finally she became angry. 'What the hell are you doing here?' she yelled at me.

I reminded her about the keys. 'I don't give a toss now,' she snarled. 'I'm glad he's dead. I hope, if it was murder, they get away with it. If he was alive now, I'd kill him anyway.'

My investigation seemed to be fast slipping away. 'Perhaps I should go,' I said, half-rising from my chair.

Her attitude changed immediately. 'No, please don't go yet,' she pleaded. 'I need someone to talk to. Someone to tell me what to do.'

I sat back down reluctantly. 'I don't think I'm the best person for that,' I said. 'You need a lawyer.'

She sighed. 'Yes, you're right.' There was reluctance in her voice but a degree of resignation. 'I needn't grieve any more for the perfect man – need I? He was a cheat and a liar. For God's sake, he even described her funeral.'

'Perhaps he was describing another funeral.'

'You're not suggesting that it was another wife's funeral – that he was a serial bigamist?'

'I'm not sure what I'm suggesting, but one funeral is very like another. Easy to describe, and perhaps he had a creative streak.'

'Obviously I didn't know him at all,' she said miserably.

'What about his belongings?'

'What about them?'

'Did the police search the house?'

'No. Why should they? The only visit we had here was from Brian Brampton. He came to offer his condolences.'

'Have you sorted out Rupert's belongings?'

She shook her head. 'I sent some of his clothes to a charity shop, but otherwise I haven't tried to sort out the paperwork yet. I just haven't felt up to it.'

I glanced at my watch. It was approaching eleven p.m. and I had to be on duty for seven thirty.

'If you want, I'll help you sort out his stuff tomorrow.'

She shrugged. 'Whatever. I'm past caring.'

Although I felt guilty at leaving her alone, she was too upset to think clearly, and I was too tired. I suggested she asked her neighbour over.

'Victor will be sound asleep. And when he hears I'm not the rich widow he thought I was, he'll see his dreams of keeping his farm disappear, and he'll ditch me.'

'You can't be sure of that.'

'Oh yes I can.' Then she added, 'I'm not cut out to be a farmer's wife anyway.'

'Has he proposed already?'

'As good as. But at the moment, in my view, all men are untrustworthy, and he says he loves me, but then so did Rupert. They just love themselves.'

'You'll feel better in the morning,' I said.

'No, I won't,' she snapped. 'The effects of the brandy will have worn off by then.'

As I drove away, I couldn't help wondering if Victor had taken advantage of her vulnerability. After all, Rupert had only died in January. Or was Victoria simply unable to cope without a man around?

I rang Hubert very early the next morning,

before I went on duty. He was barely awake. I told him about the latest development.

'What do you want to do?' he asked. 'Abandon ship?'

At that moment, I had a thumping headache. I dreaded the day ahead and I didn't know what to do next, so I didn't answer.

'Give it till your next days off,' he said. 'You can think about it then. Something will turn up.'

I wasn't convinced. 'How's Jasper?'

'He's coping. I'll give you a ring later.'

'Cheers.'

I hurried downstairs, and I was just passing the patients' lounge on Churchill Ward when I heard a whispered, *'Kate … in here.'*

'What are you doing here?' I asked Victoria. She looked ill: pale, but with swollen pink eyes. 'I've come back to work. I haven't slept all night but I'm not going to let that bastard get the better of me. I need to know everything.'

'Good for you.'

'Here, take these,' she said, thrusting a set of keys into my hand. 'Don't get caught.'

The day was fairly uneventful. Marie spent less time in the staff loo, and we managed to sort out the care plans. At lunch time, I joined Polly and a young care assistant in the cafeteria. 'Hiya, Kate,' she said cheerfully. 'You're just in time to see my Christmas photos. I've only just had a chance to get them done.' For once, I was really interested in someone's snaps.

'We had a great time,' she said. 'Just one floor kept open, so we didn't have much to do.

'This is me wearing my antlers, doing the meds,' she said, passing it to me. 'And this is me with a patient.' There were several photos of Polly posing. 'I have to get loads taken of me for my mum and dad.'

'And this is the surgical team.' I stared at the group for some time.

'And this is Mr Decker-White, is it?' I asked, pointing at the man in the middle.

'That's him. Good-looking guy, wasn't he?'

He certainly was. On looks alone, I could see why Victoria had fallen for him.

The care assistant called Kimberly murmured, 'I miss him.'

Polly smiled. 'Come on, Kim, get over it.' Then she turned to me. 'Kim had a bit of a crush on him. She thought the sun shone through—'

'Don't be such a cow, Polly. He wasn't like the others. He was always nice to me.'

'I think he fancied you.'

'No he didn't.'

I wouldn't have been surprised if he had, for Kim had a wonderful complexion, a soft sensual mouth and a pert little body. And she looked to be eighteen or nineteen years old.

'Look,' said Polly. 'What about this one of you with him?'

As the photo was passed to her, Kim looked shocked. 'When did you take this?'

'That was at the Christmas Eve bash at the Decker-Whites' place.'

Kim was about to hand it back when she said, 'What do you think, Kate?'

I stared at the photo, not just because they were in a passionate clinch, or because Rupert had his hand firmly on her bottom, but because in the background stood a man wearing a grey suit. The same man I'd seen in Louise Booth's office on my first day. They'd been arguing, but I barely remembered what was said.

'Who is that man in the background?' I asked.

Fourteen

'That's Superintendent Brampton,' said Polly. 'Not exactly grieving over his wife's death, is he?'

'What was she like?' I asked.

'Trina...? Great looker,' said Polly thoughtfully. 'But I think she wanted more than Brian could offer her.'

'In what way?' I asked.

'She was years younger than him, and she wanted some fun. Brian liked going out, but with his mates.'

'I thought she was a bit boring,' said Kim. 'Always rattling on about her weight or hair or what make-up she'd bought. Once she talked to me for fifteen minutes on the state of her nails – fingers *and* toes.'

'She's dead,' said Polly. 'She can't speak for herself, she was a good nurse and she had a kind heart.'

'What about her husband?' I asked.

Silence from both of them until Polly shrugged, saying, 'I don't know him well enough to comment.'

'Nor me,' said Kim.

They both looked uncomfortable and Polly glanced at her watch. 'I'll have to go,' she said. 'We're really busy.'

'And me,' said Kim.

The photos were gathered up and the pair of them rushed away. They still had ten minutes to spare.

I finished my shift at four and went straight to my room. All was quiet in the corridor. At my door, I turned the key but it was already open. I stared at the key – surely I hadn't forgotten to lock my door? I pushed it open and saw that my curtains were tight shut. Was I going mad? I was sure I'd opened them. Then a figure stepped into my line of vision.

'Close the door,' she said. 'I don't want anyone to know I'm here.'

'What the hell is going on, Victoria? You scared me.'

I closed the door and switched on the light. 'How did you get in here?'

'The master key ... I need to talk.'

I needed a few minutes to unwind before she started, but she had an expression on her face that was somewhere between fear and excitement, so I sat down on the bed and waited for her to explain.

'I've been working on the accounts,' she told me. 'And there is a discrepancy. A big one. I'd noticed before, but I thought I'd made a mistake. That was one of the reasons I took time off. I thought if I had a break I could sort it out.'

'But you can't? How much is missing?'

She stared at me a few moments. 'That's the point, Kate,' she murmured. 'There's nothing missing. There are amounts of money, large amounts of money, that I can't explain. I don't know its origin.'

I'm a simple soul and too much money sounded a far better deal than having a deficit.

I could see that it worried Victoria, but my competency with any sort of accounts bordered on the remedial. Hubert paid my tax online and it still remained a bit of a mystery to me.

'Do you think Rupert was putting in extra money?'

'I'm not talking a few hundred pounds,' she said irritably. 'We have a joint account and I know he had a few stocks and shares, but he must have had other accounts that I know nothing about.'

Then, as if realizing, she put her hands to her face and rocked backwards and forwards for a few moments. 'Why the hell should I be surprised?' she muttered. 'He had a wife I knew nothing about.'

'You must see a lawyer and a top-notch accountant,' I urged her. 'You can't manage this on your own.'

She sighed. 'You're right. I can't think straight. I'll do that – I'll go tomorrow.'

Although I offered to make her tea she refused, saying that she wanted to slip away without being seen and that she was going straight home. I checked the corridor to make sure it was empty and Victoria hurried away.

I was filling the kettle to make myself tea when I turned to find Suki behind me, smiling. 'I wish I was like you,' she said.

'Why?' I asked in surprise.

'You have no responsibilities,' she said.

'That's true,' I said. 'Perhaps that isn't a good thing. It makes people selfish.'

'I love my children but I cannot be with them.'

'But you *are* working hard for them and their future.'

'Yes, but I feel very sad. My husband is ill again – he may have to go into hospital.'

'I'm sorry. Is there anything I can do?'

She shook her head. 'No, I just have to wait for news.'

She wandered off, having refused my offer of tea, and I took my mug back to my room.

By eight p.m. I was in bed, with my alarm clock set for two a.m. When it did go off, I was awake instantly. I put on a black tee shirt and black jeans, thrust the keys into one pocket and a notebook and pen into the other. In my hand I carried a small torch. I crept along the corridor and then down the first flight of stairs to the doorway that led to the wards. I didn't see anyone, but my heartbeat was going into overdrive and I could hear the blood pounding in my ears. If I was caught now, torch in hand, how was I going to explain myself?

The lights were dim and I could see easily enough until I got to the administration floor. There the lights were off and the corridor was as dark as a cave. Using the torch, I managed to find Louise's office more by feel than sight. The chinking of the keys sounded, in the silence, as loud as a herd of cows wearing cowbells.

Once the door was opened, the room that now faced me had drawn blinds and no chinks of light. My torch was a mere candle in the darkness. I closed the door and felt for a light switch. The overhead strip lighting was overly bright and I worried that if the security man walked the corridor, he'd see the light under the door. It was a chance I'd have to take.

I unlocked the only filing cabinet and found the individual staff folders. I suspected that the information had also been transferred to computer, but I was grateful for the simplicity of the printed word. Each file contained personal information, CVs, references, health profiles. In the lower drawer of the cabinet, I found five years' worth of previous nursing and ancillary staff. Trina's file was missing, but there was an address on a stray slip of paper and someone had written RIP in the corner. It was fortuitous if it *was* her home address.

I began flicking through the files, not really knowing what I would find, or if it would be useful. Ward manager Marie O'Grady had a history of depression and had been prescribed Prozac. She was often off sick and had had one verbal warning about being late. Strangely, Polly's file gave her address as Fair Acres. Was that merely an oversight, or did she want to keep her home address secret? My guess was that the files, once completed, were very rarely looked at again. I wrote down a few names and addresses, but various noises startled me occasionally. Phones ringing, lifts moving. I began to feel nervous. I stuffed the notebook back in my pocket and decided to put the files back immediately. If I was caught, it would be curtains for my investigation and a trip to court.

I picked up five or so files and was about to put them back when I heard a door open with a creak close by. Clumsily I dropped two of the files. I left them on the floor and went to the door to listen. All was quiet outside, but even so I switched off the light and relied on my torch to put the files back in their correct place.

Then, stealthily, I opened the door and locked it. Guided by the torch, I was moving along the corridor when a door opened, and in a shaft of light I could see a burly uniformed figure. Worse still was that he'd seen me. Think of something, I told myself. Then I fell to the floor.

'Who's that? What you up to?' he yelled as he switched the lights on and came fast towards me.

'Thank goodness you've come,' I said dramatically as I glanced up into his round face. 'I couldn't find the light switch and I'm desperate. I've lost my contact lens.' I cast the torch light over the carpet in a demented fashion.

'Down 'ere?' he said suspiciously.

'I've looked everywhere else where I was in the day.'

'You only got the one pair?'

'I've run out. I'm new here and I haven't had a chance to get to an optician's.'

'Which ward are you working on?'

'Churchill. Will you help me? I can only see with one eye.'

'Yeah, alright,' he said reluctantly. 'Couldn't you have looked earlier?'

'I did. This is the last place I could think of. I fell asleep and remembered I'd been down here in the afternoon.'

From the leather belt surrounding his pot belly, he produced a torch as big as a weapon.

'Which office did you go to?' he asked.

'Miss Booth's.'

'We'll 'ave a look in there first,' he said.

Inside the office, he told me to search around the desk. With some difficulty, because of his bulk, he got on to his hands and knees and began scanning the carpet around the door. After a very short time, he said, 'Why didn't you notice you'd lost it at the time?'

This had me stumped for a moment. By now I was underneath the desk. 'They are so comfortable,' I explained, 'and I do rely on my good eye, so it wasn't until I had to read something I noticed. I had to cover my bad eye to be able to see.'

That seemed to satisfy him, and a few moments later I shouted excitedly, 'I've found it! I've found it!' Struggling to my feet with my right hand closed over my imaginary lens, I heard the security guard mutter, 'Thank Gawd for that.'

After thanking him profusely, I made a hasty exit, but at the doorway I turned and saw that he was frowning as if puzzled about something.

Back in my room, I couldn't sleep. I had a few addresses, but did that gain me any real information? The answer was, of course, no. But if I did a little surveillance, then I might at least gain a suspect. For at the moment I had only some doubts and not a single person who could have a motive for murder, except, of course, for Victoria herself.

I was drifting off to sleep when I remembered that puzzled frown of the security man, and that I'd been told Brian Brampton might have had a spy on the premises. So, was my burly guard a police informant, and if so, what information could he be relaying? More to the point, was Brampton a straight cop, or was he, as I suspected, as bent as a catapult?

The night was short and I felt bleary-eyed and confused at six thirty a.m. when my alarm went off. A quick shower and a strong coffee worked wonders, and I managed to concentrate during the morning handover. It seemed I was thought competent enough to bring back three patients from theatre. In the meantime, I was to help with bed-making and washes.

I hadn't met any of the theatre staff yet, just a glimpse of masked faces. Theatre was where I needed to work, although my career as a scrub nurse amounted to only two tonsillectomies and an appendectomy. In the NHS operating room, assistants did much of the technical work, such as setting up the various machines and cameras, but I knew nothing of the theatre set-up at Fair Acres. I resolved to ask if there were any vacancies, although I had the feeling the answer would be no. Operating staff, in my experience, tend to keep themselves separate from mere ward staff. They shower and change separately, eat and make their own hot drinks, and rarely visit the cafeteria. Theirs is a complete little world, except, of course, when it comes to a party.

During my lunch break, I rang Victoria on her mobile. There was no reply. I tried again at tea time. I didn't dare go down the administration corridor again to find out if she'd actually been working, so I left it till six p.m. and rang her at home on her landline. There was still no reply.

Fifteen

I was a little concerned about Victoria not answering her phone, but not worried. Not, that is, until I rang Hubert. He was all doom and gloom. 'You just be careful if you go out. It's snowing here. The roads will be treacherous.'

'It's not snowing here,' I said. Not that I actually knew, because I hadn't managed to open my curtains yet. I tweaked them back and saw that it was just beginning to snow, the sky was growing dark and the beginnings of frost lent an air of foreboding to the coming night.

'It's forecast all over the Midlands,' he said. 'Why don't you leave it until David comes to see you?'

'I'm a big girl now. And how are you, Hubert? And how's Jasper?'

'We're fine. Don't change the subject. Remember the near misses you've had in the past.'

'I try hard to forget. If I did remember, I'd

wrap myself in a shawl and sit down in a rocking chair.'

'There's no need to get shirty. Have a word with David.'

'What's he doing there?'

'We're having a drink. I'll hand you over.'

'Hi. How's it going?' asked David.

'Fine,' I murmured, somewhat distracted by his being with Hubert. It all seemed a bit cosy to me.

'I hear you're planning a trip out this evening.'

'It's not a "trip out", as you put it. I am meant to be investigating a murder.'

'You could be wasting your time if it was an accident.'

'I could,' I said pointedly. 'But I don't think I am.'

'Hubert's right,' he said. 'Weather conditions are set to deteriorate, and that includes *all* parts of the Midlands.'

'I'll think about it. I'll take a torch, blanket and shovel if I do go out.'

David's silence spoke volumes. 'Are you still there?' I asked.

'Yes,' he said coldly. 'I've got a name and address for you, but I'm not sure now that I should give them to you.'

'Tell me and I promise I won't go out if the weather worsens.'

148

'I was planning to come and see you on Thursday,' he said, 'but I can't make it. Half the station is off with a flu bug and Hubert's on a conveyor belt that won't stop.'

Secretly I was relieved.

'Write this down,' he said. 'Brett Yule, 24 Water Lane, Little Makham. He's been in trouble before.'

'For violence?'

'No, taking and driving away.'

'You're an angel.'

'No I'm not. I'm a bloody fool, but you'd find out anyway – and if anyone at Fair Acres finds out who you are, you could be in real trouble.'

It was the guarded tone of his voice, not just his words, that worried me. 'You know something, don't you, and you're not telling me?'

'Don't underestimate the local police, Kate, and watch your back.'

'Is it about—?' I began, but he didn't let me finish.

'That's all I'm saying. The matter is closed. Just keep in touch and take care.'

I put down the phone reluctantly and went to the window. The snow fell now fast and furious, with big flakes that would settle quickly. If I *was* going, it was best I went straight away. I tried Victoria one more time, both on her landline and mobile. I left messages then dressed warmly and waited a further ten minutes. I guessed she was with her neighbour but it still worried me.

The first few miles towards Upper Tapston was slow due to the volume of home-going traffic, but then the traffic thinned and I was virtually alone. The snow became heavier still, and my windscreen wipers could hardly cope. My speed dropped to twenty miles an hour and I regretted ever setting out. You are a stupid bitch, I told myself, but it was too late to turn back now, and I'd have to drive sensibly and keep my nerve.

Eventually I reached The Pines and, seeing the house lights were ablaze, I felt reassured. If I was trapped by the snow, at least I'd be comfortable.

I knocked loudly at the front door and rang the doorbell. There was no response. I tried at the back door and again there was no response. I tried the door handle. Once again, she'd left the back door open. The smell of a casserole cooking permeated the kitchen. I opened the oven door to see a terracotta crock pot on the bottom shelf in a very low oven. Oven gloves were placed neatly on the work surface. I carefully took out the crock pot and glanced inside. I turned off the cooker, for whatever it was had been cooking for a very long time.

Checking every room, there was no sign of Victoria, but her bed hadn't been made, which in itself didn't indicate much, except that maybe she'd been in a hurry to get the substantial casserole in the oven, ready for lunch – or was it supper? Either way it would feed two people. It was time to visit her neighbour.

I tramped through the snow, clutching my largest torch, out of her back garden via a gate that led to a field. In good weather it would have been an average-size field. In blizzard-like conditions, it seemed to me to be as vast as the Russian steppes. Don't exaggerate, I told myself, as I brushed the snow that swept into my face and hair. Unlike the Russian steppes, a few hundred yards away, the house lights of Victoria's neighbour glimmered. An unlikely pairing, I thought – Victoria and a farmer.

A dog barking excitedly greeted my arrival, soon to be followed by a man, younger than I expected, who opened the door and ushered me in with the words, 'Down, Prince!'

Prince, a handsome German Shepherd, obediently lay on the floor, tail wagging. 'He loves women. Not too keen on men, but otherwise gentle as a spaniel.'

'You must be Victor,' I said, as he insisted

on helping me off with my wet jacket.

'No,' he said, smiling. 'That was a little joke of Vicky's. My name is Dale Dutchman. She liked neither the Dale nor the Dutchman. So she called me Victor.'

He and Prince led me through to a kitchen well warmed by an open coal fire, where he sat me down on a padded carver chair near the fire and handed me a towel to wipe my face and hair. He also helped me take my boots off.

The kitchen felt homely, with newspapers and *Farmer's World* magazines spread over a solid pine table. On a Welsh dresser, an assortment of odd crockery had been placed at random on the shelves. Prince, sitting at my feet, added to the homely feel.

'You must be Kate the private eye,' he said.

'How did you know?'

'Who else would be fool enough to come out in this weather?'

I looked at him properly for the first time. He didn't seem the usual farming type. Slim and tall, with clear skin, longish fair hair and deep-set blue eyes, he managed to looked more a poet than a farmer. I guessed his age at late thirties.

'Is Victoria here?' I asked. 'Her lights are on but there's no sign of her.'

He looked puzzled. 'No, she's not here. I

must admit, I did stay with her last night, but I left at the crack of dawn to feed the chickens.'

'You haven't seen her since?'

He shook his head. 'Have you tried her mobile?'

'Yes, and her landline.'

'I hope she hasn't done anything stupid,' he muttered.

'Why should she?'

He shrugged. 'We had a bit of a row. She said I was only after her money so that I could keep the farm going. I run a chicken farm, organic. Not big, but big enough for me. I'm not overly ambitious any more.'

'You were once?'

'Oh yes. I worked in the stock exchange. Made lots of money, but my adrenaline ran out. Here I'm happy and I still have some money in the bank, so I was a bit insulted by her suggestion.'

He insisted on making me tea then, and provided me with chocolate biscuits.

'Was her car there?' he asked.

I paused, trying to remember. 'No, it wasn't.'

'I'd better go and check her garage.'

'I'll do that when I go back,' I said.

'No I'll go ... just in case.'

He began pulling on a pair of muddy green

wellies, then a black padded jacket with a hood, and finally he thrust a mobile phone into the pocket. Prince, meanwhile, had got to his feet, but he didn't look that keen, as his tail was down. 'Stay, Prince,' he said. Prince resumed his position at my feet. 'He hates snow,' Dale explained. 'He was abandoned in the snow as a puppy.'

As he opened the back door, a gust of snow wafted in and Prince whined and I shivered. Crossing the field would take him less than five minutes. The fire was dying down now, so I gave it a poke and, using the tongs from the coal scuttle, I added a few more lumps of coal. Then I spent the waiting minutes stroking Prince, staring at the flames and listening to the ticking of the clock on the mantelpiece. It was old-fashioned and homely, and if being a farmer's wife meant coal fires and a friendly dog lying at my feet, maybe the life of a farmer's wife would suit me.

The minutes ticked by and I became less relaxed. Victoria's disappearance was beginning to seem very sinister. Did she think merely leaving the lights on would deter intruders, or had she been forced to leave the house in a hurry – maybe in panic? I should have checked the garage for her car, but my life as a PI was full of 'should haves', and if the engine had been running, I would have heard it. She'd been angry and worried but she hadn't appeared suicidal.

Prince left my side, tail wagging. I listened but I could hear nothing, then, minutes later, I heard the stamping of boots outside the back door. Dale appeared, covered in snow and looking grim. 'The car's there but there is no sign of her,' he said taking off his jacket and shaking it at the doorway. He wiped his face with his hands and patted Prince. 'She hasn't taken anything with her as far as I can see,' he said. 'Except for her favourite leather handbag. I think we ought to call the police.'

'Could she have walked to a friend's house?'

'Even for her nearest friend in the village, she would have taken the car.'

'It might be worth ringing her friend.'

He nodded. 'I've got her number somewhere. I went to dinner there once. She's a young widow. Women have a penchant for wanting to feed me.'

He rummaged for a while under the newspapers on the table and eventually found his diary. There was no phone in the kitchen, so I heard nothing of the call, but when he returned he looked dejected. 'Dorinda hasn't heard from Vicky in a week. She has no ideas. We'll have to phone the police.'

'That is the best thing to do,' I said, 'but do you mind leaving me out of it? Victoria wants me to investigate her husband's death, and I haven't done that yet. I want to get back to work tomorrow acting normally.'

'OK. I'll ring, but in these conditions they could be some time. I think you should stay here. I have a spare room. Think about it.'

I did think about it, but I didn't know him and I didn't want to be far from my car, because my car gave me independence, and I could go back and start up the engine and make sure it didn't freeze up.

He smiled at me. 'While you're thinking, let me make you a bite to eat.'

When he returned from calling the police, he looked thin-lipped and angry. 'They certainly won't be out here tonight. They say tomorrow at the earliest, depending on weather conditions. She has to be missing twenty-four hours at least, and black ice has caused many accidents. It's a question of priorities ... et cetera.'

'I'm not surprised,' I said. 'Missing adults are not top of their list.'

Dale set about making me cheese on toast and a mug of cocoa, while he drank single malt whisky.

'Do you know Vicky well?' he asked as he watched the grill.

'I don't know her at all really. Just that she'd been married to Rupert for three years...' I paused, wondering if he knew about Rupert's bigamy.

'She told me last night about her visit from the "other" wife.'

'You don't sound very surprised.'

He handed me the cheese on toast and sipped his single malt. 'I'm not. I always thought Rupert was low life. Being a surgeon cuts no ice with me. My father was a surgeon – and a hard, arrogant bastard he was too. Rupert was all surface looks and charm. Vicky couldn't see that – she saw only status, breeding and money.'

'Why do you think that was?'

'Her background, I suppose,' said Dale thoughtfully.

'What was her background?'

'Dirt-poor, by all accounts. Deserted by her father, with a mother who was loving but feckless. Vicky was bright and, encouraged by her teachers, she won a scholarship to a private school.'

'Did she mention her first marriage?'

'Only to say he was a rich alcoholic and she'd married too young.'

'Is he still alive?'

'They divorced and two years later he was killed in a car accident driving six times over the limit.'

I finished my supper and glanced at my watch. It was nine p.m. My car was parked outside The Pines, so I had to reclaim that, and I wasn't happy about driving back in a blizzard.

'I'll go now,' I said. 'I can make an early start in the morning if the snow isn't too deep.'

'I'd rather you stayed here,' he said. 'I'll probably sit up all night worrying.'

'You're very fond of her, aren't you?'

'More than fond,' he said. I waited for him to say more, but he didn't. Somewhat reluctantly, he helped me into my damp jacket and I slipped my boots on and then pulled up my hood. He slipped a piece of postcard into my hand. 'My mobile number. Ring me when you get to the house, and ring anytime if you have any news...' He broke off. 'There were no footprints,' he said, 'other than yours and mine.'

'She must have left before the snow started,' I said.

'If she did, she was wearing her bedroom slippers – they're missing.'

Sixteen

That remark gave me something to think about as I battled head down through the snowy field. The house lights were less comforting now, like a candlelit pumpkin – bright but hollow.

I brushed some of the snow from the windscreen of my car and switched on the ignition. Finally, on the third attempt, it started up. I let it run for a while and then switched off, but I didn't bother to lock it, there seemed no point.

Once inside the kitchen, I couldn't stop shivering. I locked the back door but left all the lights on. I wanted no shadowy corners to frighten me. I went straight upstairs and ran a hot bath.

Afterwards, in the guest room, wearing one of Victoria's towelling dressing gowns, I rang Dale to tell him that I was staying the night at the Pines, and then I rang Hubert. It was ten fifteen, David had gone home and Hubert was already in bed and sounded weary. I told him I was staying at Victoria's house for the night and, weather permitting, I'd be back at Fair Acres in the morning. He didn't pay much attention to that, but said cheerfully, 'David's agreed to be best man. Will you—?'

I didn't let him finish. 'I'm sorry, but I can't be a bridesmaid or a maid of honour.'

'I thought you'd be glad,' he said, sounding hurt, 'that I'd found the woman of my dreams.'

'That's the point, Hubert – she's not real. How can she be real if you haven't met her?'

'We communicate – maybe not face to face, but we do talk.'

I knew by the tone of his voice that I'd upset him, so I made a hasty exit. 'It's late,' I said. 'We're both tired. Give Jasper a kiss for me.'

The silence after the call was deafening. I kept the hall light on, and as I snuggled down under the duvet, my arm crept out to switch off the bedside light. Then I waited for the warmth of the duvet and the darkness of the room to lull me to sleep.

I was still waiting at midnight and one a.m. I kept imagining Victoria like a demented Cathy calling for Heathcliff on the moors. Was she out there in the fields alone? Why hadn't Dale suggested looking for her? Why indeed hadn't I suggested it? Was it too late? I sat up in bed, switched on the light and then went to the window. The snow had stopped and lay gleaming like some exotic carpet, whilst, above, the stars seemed brighter than usual. Perhaps she'd taken shelter somewhere, in a barn or an outhouse. If she was drunk, perhaps she'd fallen asleep. The thought also occurred to me that where else would she go on foot but Dale's place? But in her slippers?

I pulled on my underwear and jumper, collected my jeans, which I'd put over a radiator, and went downstairs. My jacket was hanging over the arm of a kitchen chair and was far too damp to wear, so I decided to give it ten minutes in the tumble dryer. Meanwhile, I put the kettle on and went to the fridge for the milk.

I opened the fridge door to peer inside. The fridge light switched on. Inside, eyes open and staring, a contorted Victoria look-ed back at me. Blood had trickled from her mouth and ears. The shock was like a blow to the head. I managed to close the fridge door but my knees buckled and I found myself panting for air on the kitchen floor. I felt faint and began to heave. I couldn't move. My back was against the fridge door and it felt safer that way, as if she might fall on me or, like some sort of demon, attack me. How long I sat there I didn't know. I wasn't capable of moving. I'd seen dead bodies in the past – mostly those who'd died peacefully of natural causes, not grotesquely forced into a fridge. I told myself to breathe deeply, that I had to get a grip.

Gradually I became calmer and eased myself up the fridge door. Upright, I still felt a little faint, but I managed to walk to the back door and take gulps of the bitingly cold air. After a while, I noticed I was shivering and quickly shut the door. The cold air did help a little, and I picked up my mobile phone from the kitchen table. Although my hand trembled, I was able to dial nine-nine-nine. When I spoke to the operator, I tried to keep my voice level, but even to my own ears it sounded strange, wavering and high-pitched, and I'd only managed the one word – 'Police.'

Eventually a calm female voice said, 'Police. Your name and address?' I took a deep breath, fighting the urge to babble incoherently. 'There's been a murder here. I've found the body. She was reported missing this evening.'

'Stay calm,' said the voice, as if she knew me. 'Are you sure it's murder?'

'She's wedged in the fridge.'

'A child?'

'No, a woman. It's a huge fridge.' There was a pause and I thought for a moment she didn't believe me. 'The murderer must have removed the shelves,' I said.

There was another short pause. 'Keep the line open. Are you alone?'

'Yes ... No, there's a neighbour.'

'With you?'

'No – please just send someone.'

'Bear with me. A lorry has jack-knifed causing a pile-up on the road to Upper Tapston. It might be a while before the police can get to you. The road has been closed in both directions.'

'I want to get out of here.'

'Of course you do. There's black ice everywhere and it's minus four degrees. Stay where you are. Make yourself a cup of hot, sweet tea.'

'The milk is in the fridge.'

'Oh ... Stay on the line and I'll check out that missing person report on the computer.'

Seconds later, she said, 'Only one person reported missing so far tonight. A wife reported her husband missing and he's been found dead in his car.'

I stiffened. *Oh my God!*

'Are you still there?' she asked.

'Yes. I've just realized that the murderer is

just across the field.'

'You're sure?'

'He said he'd reported her missing. He'd had a row with her earlier on. He'd spent the night here...' I broke off, thinking I'd heard something outside. I moved to the back door and listened and heard nothing.

'Does he know where you are?'

'Of course he does.'

'All right. Just do as I say and you'll be fine. Lock all the doors. Barricade yourself in and stay put. I'll do my best to get someone to you. I promise.'

Somehow I'd never trusted anyone quite so much as this anonymous operator. Apart, that is, from Hubert.

'I'll have to put the phone down now,' I said, placing it on a work surface and then moving a chair under the door handle. I ran to the front door. There was only a flimsy glass-topped table in the hall. I found a white bucket chair in the sitting room and carried that through and wedged it up against the door. Dale Dutchman might be thin, but forcing Victoria into the fridge needed strength. A chair might not be enough to keep him out.

I picked up my mobile. My saviour was waiting for me. 'All secure?' she asked. 'Are you feeling calmer?'

'Yes. I'm getting there.'

'Someone will be there as soon as they can. I've got to get off the line now, because it's chaos everywhere. Is there a room you can lock from the inside?'

'The bathroom.'

'Go there and stay there. Keep your mobile with you and I'll ring you back as soon as I can.'

Even as I spoke the words, I knew they sounded pathetic. 'They will be here before dawn, won't they?' I asked.

'Take a heavy saucepan to the bathroom with you. It'll make you feel more secure.'

Four burly armed cops would just about make me feel secure, but it was a good idea, so I thanked her anyway.

'What's your name?' I asked.

'Pearl.'

'Mine's Kate. Thanks again, Pearl.'

I searched the cupboards and eventually found the right cupboard. I chose a cast-iron medium-sized saucepan. It was wrist-breakingly heavy, and with a good overhead thrust would easily fell the average man – a man just like Dale.

Upstairs in the bathroom I was lucky that there was a white wicker stool by the bath. It was slightly more comfortable than sitting on the loo seat. By now it was three thirty a.m. – nearly four hours before dawn. My trusty head buster was on the floor at my feet, but the hours stretched ahead. Pearl hadn't made any promises about the police coming before dawn, and now that I was behind a locked door, I couldn't bear the thought of spending hours thinking and growing more and more nervous. I felt trapped when I should have felt safe.

It took half an hour for me to decide to go downstairs to the drinks cabinet. Collecting a bottle of brandy and a brandy glass, I then took a couple of novels from beside Victoria's unmade bed and made my way back to the bathroom.

I would have preferred a mug of hot sweet tea but a double brandy did seem to steady me. I stared at my mobile, desperately wanting to speak to either Hubert or David, but what could they do except worry about me? It wouldn't have been fair on them. I tried to read but the words meant nothing. Occasionally I heard sounds outside, but I couldn't distinguish them. My mind seemed blank, except for the recurring sight of Victoria. I'd hardly known her, but I'd just begun to actually like her, and although I would have preferred to go home, I knew that I'd fulfil my promise to her, because that was all that was left.

Depression settled over me like the snow. It seeped into my soul. Life was dark and dangerous. People were evil ... Now come on, I told myself, only a few people were evil. I thought of Dale Dutchman. An odd name for an odd man, but he hadn't seemed evil. In fact, whilst I was with him, he looked, behaved and sounded normal. I supposed that was how serial killers remained un-detected, to kill and kill again. But then, if Dale had killed just the once, wouldn't I have noticed something in his demeanour – either excitement or some degree of agita-tion? You're not that clever, my inner voice told me. At least, I wasn't that stupid either, because I hadn't stayed the night there.

I drank another brandy, knowing it wasn't wise, knowing I should keep my wits about me, but the bottle was there, I was alone and anxious, and that was excuse enough.

I glanced at my watch. Only an hour had passed. I felt very tired now, and for the first time, I looked at the bath with new eyes. On a stainless steel open shelf were enough towels for a B&B. Fluffy towels of all sizes, but colour-coordinated. I laid the smaller ones for a pillow, put several on the bottom of the bath and covered myself with three bath sheets. I clambered in, holding the saucepan. As I lay down and began to drift off to sleep, my spirits lifted. My bath bed seemed almost luxurious and, when it came, sleep seemed like a gift from the gods.

How long my sleep lasted I didn't know, but I did know that someone was walking upstairs. No, not walking – striding. As I staggered to my feet, I slipped on the towels and the cast-iron pot crashed on to my foot. The pain took my breath away, and when the footsteps stopped outside the bathroom door, I screamed out, partly in pain, but mostly in fear. 'Keep out! I've got a weapon. The police are on their way.'

'Kate. It's me, Dale,' he said softly. 'There's nothing to be afraid of. Open the door.'

Seventeen

As I stood by the bathroom door, I could see blood seeping through the foot of my tights. It hurt like hell, but the threat was outside and I had to concentrate on that. He was trying the handle now. 'What's happened? Why are you frightened of me? What's going on?'

The bastard would easily win a place at RADA. I didn't answer, as I struggled to fit my boot on my injured foot. I reasoned it would give my foot some support if I had to make a run for it, but I winced in pain and swore under my breath.

'I'm going downstairs now,' he said. 'I'll make a cup of tea. I'll pass one in to you if you want.'

You'll be lucky, I thought.

I heard him go downstairs and, moments later, with my ear pressed to the door, I could hear the slight noise of running water. Then there was silence. A watched kettle never boils, neither does one listened to. My nerve endings were beginning to twitch and my foot throbbed. A crashing sound made me jump back from the door. I waited for more noise, but minutes passed and downstairs all was silent. Should I leave the bathroom or not? Then, before I'd had time to decide, my mobile rang. It was Pearl.

'You're OK,' she said. 'Thank goodness. I've tried you twice. The police are on their way – they should be with you soon.'

I didn't tell Pearl he was in the house, because there was nothing she could do to help me now. Judging by the noise he'd made, he might well have rushed out of the house. Perhaps he was finding an axe to batter down the door? If so, I would rather be on the rampage, with my adrenaline running and my saucepan raised, than cowering in fear in a locked bathroom.

My foot throbbed, but I could walk, and I made my way slowly and quietly down the stairs towards the kitchen. I heard only my own footsteps and the blood thumping in my ears. I half expected him to charge at me like some deranged madman in a horror film, but I saw nothing and heard nothing.

I peered round the kitchen door. The fridge door was open and there on the expensively tiled floor was Dale – out cold – in a pool of blood, vomit, tea and broken pieces of crockery. Just for a moment, I thought he too was dead, but then he began to groan. I swung the door of the fridge closed, averting my eyes, and then frantically searched the cupboards for tea towels or tablecloths. He was bleeding heavily from a cut above his eye, and his face was a greyish white. He'd obviously keeled over sideways and cracked the side of his head. I turned his head to get a better look at the wound. It was a clean-looking gash that would need suturing, but as we say in the trade, there were no 'foreign bodies', so, using a clean, ironed tea towel, I applied pressure to the bleeding point.

'You bitch,' he muttered. 'You could have warned me.'

I laughed briefly, partly from relief, partly from hysteria. 'I thought you were the murderer.'

He stared at me in disbelief and started to tremble. He really was in shock. I put his left hand over the tea-towel dressing and told him not to move. Not that he looked capable of moving. Then I rushed upstairs for a pillow and a duvet. Once he was covered up, I picked up the pieces of broken mug and mopped up the various fluids. 'The police are going to be here soon,' I said. 'They'll take you to hospital. They'll be quicker than an ambulance.'

'My hip hurts,' he said. He rolled on to his back and I undid his trousers and looked at his hip. There was no fat over his hip bones but there was severe bruising.

'I could do with a drink,' he said miserably. 'I feel a real wimp. It was such a bloody shock.'

'Better not drink anything,' I said, 'in case you need anaesthesia.'

'Poor Victoria,' he murmured.

Ten minutes later, the sound of a vehicle arriving raised both our spirits. We could finally get out of this place. We waited for them to appear but after a few minutes I grew impatient and went outside, to find two uniformed cops in a police car, one of whom was talking on the car phone. They both looked barely past school-leaving age. The one nearest the passenger door got out and tried to bundle me into the back of the car. 'Hang on!' I said shrugging him off. 'There's a man inside who needs help.'

'If he's armed,' said my would-be saviour, 'we'll have to wait for back-up.'

'No. He's not armed. He passed out and he's cracked his head open. He needs to get to hospital.'

'Have you called an ambulance?'

'I thought you'd be quicker.'

After I'd briefly explained the situation, the PC in the car I'd already nicknamed 'Baby Face' relayed the information back to base whilst I stood shivering. Then they took an arm each and helped me back across the snow, which crunched underfoot, and into the kitchen.

Blood had soaked through Dale's makeshift pressure dressing, and it was obvious Baby Face was squeamish, for he immediately sat down at the kitchen table. The other PC was tall and gangly, with high cheekbones and a slightly startled look. Neither of them *could* have been long out of training school. Baby Face had taken out his notebook and a pen. 'Now then, love,' he said. 'Let's have a few names.'

'I'm Kate Kinsella; the man bleeding on the floor is Dale Dutchman. He runs the chicken farm nearby.'

'I'm PC Norton and my tall friend is PC Hounslow.'

I nodded and made another tea-cloth pad for Dale's wound. The bleeding had nearly stopped and Dale's colour had improved to a vaguely normal hue. 'I'm fine now,' he said. 'But I feel a right prat lying here.'

'Stay where you are,' I said. 'The ambulance won't be long.'

'Ha. Ha. Ha,' he responded, and I could

only agree.

'Is he all right?' asked Norton.

'Yes, he'll be fine,' I said. 'I'm a nurse. There's more blood than cut.'

'Where's the body then?' he asked.

I pointed towards the fridge. 'She's in there. Victoria Decker-White.'

'They told me it was in a freezer,' said Norton. 'Will you have a look, Rich?'

PC Hounslow, manfully squaring his shoulders, went to the fridge door. He opened it a mere fraction, but that was enough to make him step backward with his mouth open.

'I take it the forensics team won't be wasting their time then?' said Norton laconically.

An hour later, following interminable questions and laboriously written notes, the ambulance arrived. Two cheerful paramedics came in, one short and middle-aged, the other a slight-looking woman in her twenties. Dale was taken out in a wheelchair and, seeing me limping, the woman said, 'I'm Debbie. Come with me to be checked over. You look all in ... and what's wrong with your foot?'

I told her about the cast-iron pan. 'Health hazard they are. Sue the company.'

I think she was joking.

We left PCs Norton and Hounslow to wait

for the forensics team and CID, and they chose to do that sitting in the police car. 'Rich' Hounslow had kindly offered to drive my car back to Fair Acres for me. With so much going on, I hadn't given the car a thought, and I was very grateful because I guessed it was an exception to some sort of police rule. They waved to us cheerfully as the ambulance drove away.

The journey to the nearest hospital with an A&E was slow, even slower was the hour's wait outside in the A&E car park. We were not top priority, merely walking wounded, and the snow had caused numerous accidents.

I rang Fair Acres and told Louise Booth I wouldn't be in. I didn't mention Victoria; I thought that was a job for the police, and it would have created too many questions. I knew that eventually the police would find out I was a PI, but I'd already decided to say that I'd given up my agency and was working as a care assistant before deciding to go on a back-to-nursing course. There did remain the question of how I happened to know Victoria Decker-White. I mulled over that for ages, and was still deliberating with myself when we were allowed into A&E.

The triage nurse saw us first. She warned me I might have a long wait. What a surprise!

Dale was behind curtains within fifteen minutes and was soon being wheeled off for a skull X-ray.

I sat for another two hours, but at least the houseman who came to examine my foot was young and good-looking with a gentle touch. The first real view of my foot came as a shock. It was black and the skin had torn. It looked mangled. 'That'll need an X-ray,' he said.

'What about working?' I asked.

He looked surprised. 'No weight-bearing for a week at least, unless you've got a desk job. And no driving, but let's see what the X-ray tells us first.'

The X-ray revealed a bit of a chipped bone, but all I'd need was the wound cleaned, a dressing and bandage and a pair of crutches. While I waited for a nurse, I hobbled outside to use my mobile. I didn't want to spend a week stuck in a room at Fair Acres. Hubert's mobile was switched off, so I assumed he was at a funeral, but David answered his. I merely told him I had a foot injury and couldn't drive. Could he pick me up from Fair Acres? Any time would do.

'Could be nine o'clock tonight,' he said. 'So how did it happen?'

'I'll tell you when I see you. Thanks for helping me out.'

'Pleasure. But be ready to tell me all.'

That sounded ominous, but again I was more than grateful.

I took a taxi back to Fair Acres and luckily my emergency twenty pound note, kept inside my bra for such a contingency, just covered the cost. Keeping money in my bra was the only useful piece of advice my mother ever gave me. Once a fiver had been enough, now twenty pounds was the minimum. The taxi driver escorted me to the door as I hobbled on my crutches, but by now the snow had turned to slush and it wasn't so treacherous. There was no sign yet of my car.

Although I was a novice on elbow crutches, I did manage the stairs unaided, but I decided that, on making an exit, I'd do it on my backside and bump my way down.

I sank on to my bed totally exhausted. I slept dreamlessly but woke with a thumping headache and the desire for gallons of tea. Slowly I made my way to the kitchen. Suki and Lorna stared at me in amazement. 'What happened to you?' asked Lorna.

'Dropped a cast-iron saucepan on my foot,' I said. I didn't want to elaborate, and they insisted they'd sort me out tea. Lorna followed me back to my room.

'You look terrible,' she said. 'Did you know

you've got blood in your hair?' I didn't, of course. Looking in a mirror hadn't been a priority.

She insisted I got back into bed, having plumped up my pillows, propped up my crutches and guided me into bed. Already I felt a patient-like dependency, and it felt good and safe. Suki arrived a few minutes later with sandwiches and tea. They both stayed to watch over me. I knew they wanted all the details – like where, when, how and why – but I didn't want to talk. My headache improved after the tea and sandwiches, and I was about to say that I wanted to sleep when, with no warning at all, there was banging at my door and a gruff male voice shouted, 'CID. Open up!'

Eighteen

Lorna looked at me with an expression of shock, and even Suki's usual calm expression gave way to an anxious frown.

'Come on,' said another voice. 'Open the bloody door.'

Lorna gave an exasperated sigh, then stood up slowly and opened the door. She took up most of the door space.

'There's no need to shout,' she snapped. 'What do you want?'

From the bed, I couldn't see their faces, but I imagined them taking a step backwards at the very least.

'We want to ask Miss Kinsella a few questions.'

'Not now, sunshine. She's not well enough, so if her car was parked in the wrong place or she's been speeding, it'll have to wait.'

'It's a murder enquiry.'

Lorna's head turned to look at me, as if to check I was still ordinary old Kate.

'Just a few questions,' said the same voice.

'Are you up for that, Kate?' asked Lorna.

'I'll be fine. Thanks.'

Lorna and Suki left then, looking slightly sheepish, and the two men came into my room.

The older one looked like my idea of a KGB agent gleaned from the cinema of my youth. Square-headed, broad-shouldered, with close-cropped grey hair and wearing a dark-grey suit, he said, 'I'm Detective Sergeant Andrew North, and my colleague here is DC Jason Maybrick – we call him Brick for short.'

I would have liked to have made some kind of retort to that, but, lying down, I felt at a disadvantage, and I obviously wanted them on my side. 'Brick' reminded me of a greyhound: thin, sleek and alert. North was more of a ponderous bulldog. North sat down in the only chair available and Brick perched gingerly on the end of my bed. With notebooks at the ready, the first few questions were merely to affirm my name, home address and next of kin. Then North moved on to the day in question. 'Why did you go to The Pines in such bad weather?'

'I didn't think the weather would deteriorate quite so much.'

'Didn't you listen to the weather forecast?'

'No. I didn't. I'd promised her the day before that I'd visit.'

'Why did she want to see you?'

'She was lonely, I suppose.'

I knew the crunch question was coming, and that I'd have to wing it. It was Brick who put the question. 'Did you meet Mrs Decker-White here?'

'No ... I met her years back – only once. She knew my mother. I think they met playing tennis or something. She recognized me when we passed in a corridor.'

I thought I'd been sharp on this one. Victoria was dead and my mother, even if she was found, would be delighted to know someone with a double-barrelled name. I reasoned that, as I hadn't yet cashed Victoria's cheque, they couldn't form a connection there. I just hoped my name wasn't in one of her cheque stubs.

'You say she was lonely,' said Brick. 'What was her mood like?'

'She was a bit down, but she had recently been bereaved.'

'Yeah, so down that she was shagging the next-door neighbour,' sneered North.

'Grief can make people act out of character. She was obviously looking for comfort.'

'Didn't find it with him, did she?' Again there was a sneer in his voice.

'He seemed very fond of her,' I said sharply. 'He was as shocked as I was to ... find her.'

181

'What time did you arrive at the house?' asked Brick gently. I supposed if they were playing good cop, bad cop, he was the good guy.

'About six, I think.'

'You're not sure?'

'No.'

He flicked back a page in his notebook. 'You told the police operator that Dale Dutchman had reported Mrs Decker-White missing.'

'Yes, he told me he had done so.'

'And what did you think when you found out he hadn't?'

'I thought he was the murderer.'

'What changed your mind?'

'His reaction when he found the body.'

'And that was?'

'Total shock. He passed out on the tiled floor, hit his head, and when I found him he was barely conscious and bleeding heavily.'

'Until that moment you thought he was the killer?'

'Yes ... but...'

'Yes or no will do,' said North.

'I'm not in court,' I said.

'You are a material witness,' he said slyly. 'So that's where you're likely to land up.'

It wasn't something I'd thought about, and now it filled me with dread.

'Tell me about arriving at Mr Dutchman's farm,' said Brick. 'What was his mood like?'

'He seemed ... normal. He wasn't agitated. He was worried about Victoria.'

'But not worried enough that he suggested looking for her?'

'I only thought that was odd afterwards, but not at the time, in the dark and the snow.'

'You didn't think about looking for her?'

I could feel a slight blush of guilt begin in my neck. 'I didn't know where to look. I should have looked for her.'

'You'd have been wasting your time anyway,' said North dourly. 'What time did you open the fridge?'

'It was two in the morning. I couldn't sleep, so I got up to make tea. I went to the fridge for milk.'

Just saying the words brought back the awful image of those staring eyes and her misshapen body. I took a deep breath.

'Are you OK?' said Brick.

I nodded but I suddenly felt nauseous.

'Did the victim have any enemies that you knew of?'

'I told you. I didn't actually know her.'

He didn't give up. He was, I decided, only part greyhound – he had terrier instincts: keep digging and don't give up.

'Why not ask a friend to visit then?'

'I don't know. Maybe she wanted to speak to a virtual stranger.'

'Speak about what?'

'Your guess is as good as mine, DC Maybrick.'

Brick's mouth tightened. North nibbled the top of his biro thoughtfully. 'She'd just returned to work,' said North. 'As financial director. Now, supposing there was a problem with the accounts...'

'I'm hardly numerate,' I interrupted him. It was a mistake. He looked at me sharply.

'So it *is* about money?'

'I wouldn't know, but I was told that she'd recently had a visit from her husband's first wife.'

North cast me a glance of real suspicion. 'Why didn't you tell us this before?'

'I've only just remembered. I have spent hours in A&E and I'm in pain. I think I'm doing quite well. I am trying to be helpful.'

'So who told you about this visit?'

'Dale Dutchman.'

'And what exactly did this first wife want with the victim? Not to offer her condolences, I take it?'

'Hardly,' I said. 'She came to tell Victoria that she wasn't dead at all.'

'Bigamy?'

'Yes.'

North turned to Brick. 'There we are then. That's the motive. Money. First wife would have a claim on the estate.'

'Have you got a suspect?'

North gave me a how-stupid-can-you-be look and then smiled in a self-satisfied way.

'No worries. He'll be in custody tomorrow morning.'

'Who?' I asked.

'Dutchman, of course.'

'But you've no evidence.'

'We've got evidence. Seems he's got a psychiatric history, had treatment in a mental hospital.'

'That's prejudice. He was stressed through work. It doesn't make him a killer.'

North smiled. 'It does now, because we've already found a bloodstained murder weapon in his living room.'

I had no retort to that. I was shocked. How could I have got him so wrong?

'So, there you are Miss Kinsella. He'll admit it soon enough.'

They left then, thanking me for my help. I lay back feeling physically and emotionally exhausted, but my mind raced. Tomorrow Dale would be in custody. Somehow I had to see him before then – at the hospital. But I would need help, and even if David agreed, which I doubted, it would be difficult.

I hobbled around the room without my crutches, took two painkillers and packed my overnight bag. David would only have to make a small detour. Then I lay on the bed and waited.

He arrived just after eight thirty. 'You look pale,' he said. 'Come on, let's get you home.'

'You'd do me a favour, wouldn't you?' I wheedled as I stroked his arm.

'I've done you a favour already,' he said. 'I've driven a hundred miles to get here.'

'And I'm very grateful. Another ten miles or so wouldn't make that much difference?'

'You're manipulating me. What the hell has been going on?'

'I gave someone first aid and he's being kept in hospital and I wanted to see how he was getting on.'

David stared at me. 'You're telling lies, Kate. I can see it in your face. Come on, tell me the truth.'

Reluctantly I said, 'This patient I want to see ... he's under police guard. And I need you to flash your warrant card.'

There was a slight pause before he spoke. 'No way. It's straight home, or you can stay here.'

'Right then. I'll stay here.'

With that, David marched out of the room and slammed the door behind him.

Nineteen

David came back, angry and grudging, but five minutes later we were sitting in reception and I was under pressure once more.

'If you can put together a good enough case for seeing this man, then I'll do it,' said David.

I put my case. I tried hard to be succinct but I gabbled over some points and I could see he wasn't being convinced. 'Don't you think,' I said finally, 'that it's a bit convenient that Rupert dies, followed swiftly by his wife?'

'Coincidence maybe,' he muttered. Then he added, 'Who benefits from Victoria's death?'

'That's the point, isn't it?' I said. 'Dutchman may not have been best pleased that Victoria was not the rich widow he imagined, but killing her would make no difference. Especially as he knew the first wife had turned up.'

David looked thoughtful. I pressed home

my trump card. 'Dutchman may be nervy, but he loves his dog and his farm. I don't think he'd jeopardize his new life by killing Victoria, especially so close to home.'

'I don't trust your logic,' he said. 'But your intuition is sometimes spot on. OK. I'll do it, but you'll have to walk without crutches and pretend to be my DC. Five minutes with him, no more, while I distract the guard.'

I kissed his cheek. And murmured that I was really grateful, which I was.

I managed a long hospital corridor without hanging on to David's arm. I couldn't avoid limping, but I reasoned that if my foot worsened he'd feel guilty, so it was tit for tat really.

Dale's room door was opened and a uniformed male PC stood chatting to a pretty student nurse. Dale's eyes were closed and it was obvious the side of his head had been shaved where the wound had been sutured. David drew the young PC aside, showed him his warrant card and, after a few moments' hesitation, both he and the nurse left the room.

'What did you say?' I asked.

'I told him you were from the fraud squad, investigating insider dealing.'

Dale opened his eyes as I approached the bed. 'I've got just five minutes, Dale,' I said.

'If anyone asks, I was from the fraud squad.'

'I wish,' he said miserably. 'They think I did it. They searched my place and said they'd found the murder weapon.'

'What sort of weapon?'

'A bloodstained hammer.'

'Where did they find it?'

'In the brass coal scuttle.'

My mouth dried. 'But they couldn't have done,' I murmured.

'Don't you think I told them that?' he said bitterly. 'But they've already made up their minds that I'm a homicidal maniac.'

I thought back to the previous evening. Dale had gone to Victoria's and I'd sat watching the glow of the open fire. I hadn't been able to resist putting on an extra few lumps of coal and giving the fire a poke. I'd used the coal tongs and the poker. The only other tools were a small brass coal shovel and a brush. I knew it was called a companion set, and it had no alien members in its brass container.

'While you were out, I used the poker and the tongs,' I said. 'There *was* no hammer there then.'

'Will you tell them?'

'Of course I'll tell them,' I said. 'Try not to worry. When they question you tomorrow, make sure you have a solicitor present, and stay calm. It'll get sorted.'

'Thanks. If you get a chance, can you check on Prince for me? He's staying with Dorinda.'

'I'll do that when I can, but I'll ring her anyway.'

I wrote the number down. Dale closed his eyes and I crept away, more worried than when I'd arrived.

'Was it worth the extra hobble?' asked David as he drove away.

'I think so.'

'Well ... tell me why.'

I was reluctant to use the words – 'plant', 'fitted up' or 'framed'. How often criminals claimed those words. Sometimes it was true, but hearing about 'fit-ups' and knowing of one first hand was different and chilling. Because, who else but someone in the police force could be responsible?

I told David that there had been no bloodstained hammer in the companion set. I tried to be logical and unemotional. Until, that is, he said, after a moment's thought, 'There is a possibility that he put it there *after* you'd toyed with his fire tools.'

'Why the hell would he do that?' I asked loudly. 'That makes no sense at all. He could have buried it anywhere outside, or he could have hidden it in a barn – even in with the chickens.' I could feel my voice rising along with my emotions. Dale *was* being framed and I had to stay calm. I thought back to the time Dale returned to the kitchen. He'd made a pot of tea and grated the cheese and toasted the bread. At no time until I left his house was he out of my sight.

'So you think someone in the police force is deliberately trying to frame Dutchman so that he gets life for a murder he didn't commit?'

'Precisely.'

David slowed as we approached a village. The miles still stretched ahead and the roads were slick with residual snow, but at least they had been gritted. I tried to relax and closed my eyes, wanting to sleep, to escape from my worrying thoughts. But as I did so, the image of Victoria's dead face sprang into my brain like the same photograph in an album constantly flicking over.

'There's only one question then,' said David, with a tiny note of triumph in his voice. 'Why? What reason can you suggest for anyone bothering to take the risk of planting evidence on a chicken farmer?'

'I can think of lots of reasons,' I said. 'But one thing has occurred to me. Someone may have thought the two of them would be together at the time. Perhaps Dale should have died too. Framing him for her murder was second choice.'

There was a long pause before David said, 'Just shut up, Kate, and let me drive.'

I slept then, dreaming of road accidents and mangled bodies, but the miles passed and the next time I opened my eyes we were driving into Humberstone's car park. Bleary-eyed, I tried to focus on my wristwatch. It was midnight.

Hubert opened the door to us in his dressing gown, with Jasper wriggling in his arms. Hubert looked as crumpled as I felt. He handed me Jasper, and I burrowed my face in his soft warm neck and promptly burst into tears.

'I'm glad it wasn't me that had that effect,' said Hubert, putting an arm around me. 'You look terrible. This nursing lark is taking its toll on you.'

'If only it was just that,' I said, wiping my eyes with my hand and carrying Jasper upstairs.

Even though I had no appetite, Hubert insisted that what I really needed were bacon sandwiches and cocoa. I tried to eat, but all I wanted was to lie down and rest my foot in my own bed, with Jasper beside me.

I could see David and Hubert exchanging knowing glances, and I knew as soon as I left the room, David would be telling Hubert everything. It would at least save me the effort.

Three days later, having slept, eaten well and rested my foot, I was walking relatively normally and was keen to get back to Fair Acres. Partly because I feared they might sack me, as they had grounds, and partly because I was afraid of losing my nerve.

Hubert's attitude over our Saturday-morning breakfast was, 'Let the police do their job. They can sort it.'

I looked up from my toast and marmalade, 'Not if one of their number is corrupt and maybe a killer.'

Hubert's response was, 'You've got marmalade on your chin.'

'I'm going back tomorrow,' I said. 'I'll go by train. Two trains and a bus really, but if I start out early I'll get there late afternoon.'

'David will take you.'

'I'm not putting him out any more. He's done enough for me.'

Hubert, having poured me out another cup of tea, looked up at me. 'More than you know,' he said. 'He's been fending off the CID. They want you to make a written statement, but he's told them you're not well enough at the moment.'

'I suppose poor Dale has already been charged with Victoria's murder?'

He nodded. 'There's nothing you can do. Not on your own.'

'I don't care what you say – I'm going back today. There's a train at ten thirty.'

'All right, have it your way, but I'll take you to the station, just in case there's a cancellation.'

At ten fifteen, we set out with my crutches wrapped in several elastic bands, and with car-loving Jasper on the back seat. It wasn't long before I realized we'd taken the wrong direction. 'You've been kidnapped,' said Hubert. 'Did you really think I'd trust BR enough to get you back there? Weekend trains are a nightmare, so relax and we'll have lunch on the way.'

We stopped at a village pub that offered lunches, and while we waited for our meals to arrive, Hubert said, 'I know I'm being an old woman, but I would like to know your plans, so that I'll know what to worry about when you're away.'

I stared into space for a moment. What the hell was my next step?

'You're not sure, are you?' said Hubert.

I didn't like the hint of sympathy in his voice. 'I expect David has told you about Detective Superintendent Brampton and my suspicions.'

'David told me as much as you told him, but no doubt you're keeping something back.'

I shrugged. 'Not really. But I do want to interview the hit-and-run driver. He's on bail.'

'Do you know where he lives?'

'Yes.'

'Is it on the way to Fair Acres?'

'A village. Little Makham.'

'I'll take you there.'

I paused. Hubert looked hopeful and he wanted to help. 'That would be good. It'll save me a trip out.'

Once our meals arrived I asked about Shirley-Marie. 'The wedding is still on, I take it?'

'We've decided on August,' said Hubert with a smile. 'I've booked the venue – managed to get a cancellation.'

'Where?'

'Freshwater Manor House.'

'Wow!' I said. 'That's posh.'

'Nothing but the best for Shirley-Marie,' said Hubert.

I knew Hubert had been married briefly before, and that he still supported his ex-wife financially, but it seemed inappropriate to enquire after her now.

'Will her family be coming?' I asked, to be polite.

'About twenty at the last count.'

I hoped they wouldn't stay long, and once more I felt depressed about my future and Hubert's.

Once we'd finished our meal, there was no point in being leisurely, because Hubert couldn't drink beer, and the longer we stayed the more he would be tempted. I'd noticed he hadn't had chips with his meal – he'd opted for a dry baked potato and salmon. A sure sign he was trying to lose a bit of his waistline by D-day – the D standing in this instance for Doomsday.

The hit and run driver's home was on the edge of Little Makham, in a small council estate. Last in a short row of terraces, a black Astra was parked in the paved front garden and the curtains twitched as we drove up, almost as if we were expected. I'd barely knocked on the door when it opened. 'Thank God you've come,' said a pale, distraught-looking man in his forties. 'She's taken a turn for the worse.'

Twenty

'We're not who you think we are,' I said, but he wasn't listening, he was pushing me towards the stairs. I heard a groan from upstairs, and as I rushed up, I turned and shouted to Hubert, who was still in the hallway. 'Explain who we are. Tell him we've come to see Brett.'

The groan changed to a grunting noise that I immediately recognized. The woman who lay on the bed was red in the face, hair lank with sweat. 'Help me,' she said. 'I'm dying. I'm in terrible pain.'

'You're not going to die,' I said. 'How many weeks are you?'

She stared at me wide-eyed and puzzled. 'What the fuck...?'

Before I could say any more, she began grunting. I checked my watch to time the contractions. She grabbed my hand hard, digging her nails in. The contractions were strong and a mere three minutes between each one. When it passed, she said, still clinging on to my hand, 'Tell me it's not true. I'm frigging forty-five years old. My GP told me I had a tumour.'

'You're well into labour,' I said. 'I'll call an ambulance.'

'You bloody won't. Tell that ... frigging dope downstairs to get up here this minute.'

'What's his name?'

I didn't need to know, for just as another contraction started, she screamed out, 'Jimmy!' and I could hear him rushing up the stairs. He stood in the doorway breathing heavily and looking like a broken man. I took him by the hand and sat him down next to the bed. Very quietly, I said, 'I'll need your help. Now, hold your wife's hand – she's having a baby.' He paled and swayed. I had to put his head between his knees and shout for Hubert. More mayhem broke out when Brett rushed in past him. 'Mum – what's happening? Don't die.'

'No one is going to die. Your mum is having a baby. Brett, go downstairs *now* and make tea. And when you've done that, boil up a pair of scissors and some string.' He looked at me as if I were utterly mad, so I explained, 'We'll need to cut the cord.'

Brett fled, leaving Jimmy still pale but at least now holding his head up. 'Call an ambulance,' I said, trying to sound calm as more grunts and groans rent the air. I would have phoned myself, but my mobile was in the car.

'My Pam won't go into a hospital – she's got a phobia. Terrified she is.'

'Well, Jimmy, get me some clean towels and sheets and then ring for either a doctor or a midwife.' He looked towards his wife. 'Do it!' I yelled.

I concentrated then only on Pam. There was no way I could tell how advanced she was without looking. Hubert at that point tried to skulk away. 'Stay with me, Hubert,' I said. 'I might need help. And I need to wash my hands.' I sat him down, put Pam's hand in his and said, 'You'll be holding your baby soon.'

'I can't bloody believe this,' she said between dry lips. 'I was in the change.'

In the bathroom, I washed my hands thoroughly and took some deep breaths. I remembered that a normal birth was only normal once it was over. I prayed that this one would be normal.

With my hands raised as if I was scrubbed and gloved, I returned to the bedroom. Jimmy had found towels and sheets. 'Now then, Jimmy, go and turn up the central heating,' I said, sounding like a headmistress organizing a class monitor. 'When this baby comes, he or she will want to be warm.' Jimmy was a man in shock. He'd gone from the terror of fearing his wife was dying to the slow realization that he was about to become a father.

With Pam, we went swiftly from, 'Pant like a dog,' so that she didn't push vigorously too soon, to the 'push down into your bottom' routine. It seemed to take for ever, but eventually I could see the head. That was a real relief. If it had been a foot, it would have been a breech presentation and she might have needed a caesarean section.

Pam began cursing Jimmy. 'It's all your fault!' she screamed. 'I told you to be careful.' This was interspersed with as many swear words as I've ever heard. But her anger gave her strength, and when the next contraction came, I could see the head properly. I told her to stop pushing while I checked the cord wasn't around the neck. It wasn't, so I said softly, 'Go for it, Pam.'

The head turned slightly, as it should on her final push, and within seconds the shoulders appeared, and then finally a wonderfully plump little body. The baby's mouth moved and the sound of crying was magical. I lifted the baby on to Pam's breast, saying, 'Look, look,' but of course she was already looking, with a mixture of wonder and happiness mixed with bewilderment. Jimmy was kissing Pam, Hubert had tears in his eyes and was shaking hands with Brett. I was fighting off the urge to cry, because the labour wasn't quite over. I called for scissors and the string, and Brett rushed forward with them in the saucepan. I cut the cord in two places, one near the baby's navel and one by Mum, and waited for the placenta to descend. Quickly the placenta descended, looking complete, and I sighed with relief as I wrapped the baby in a towel. 'What is it then?' Jimmy shouted excitedly. 'It's a girl,' said Pam, mesmerized by her daughter's tiny fingers.

Jimmy punched the air, repeating, 'It's a girl,' at the top of his voice. Pam lay back exhausted but smiling. I had to wait to celebrate. I had no drug to calm down the uterus, and there is always a risk of haemorrhage, but I massaged her uterus until I could feel it stop contracting, and only then did the tears come.

Loud knocking at the door heralded the arrival of a midwife, a doctor and the neighbours from next door. It was bedlam and we were quickly ushered from the room.

Downstairs, Jimmy was opening cans of lager and offering them round, and the two bemused neighbours joined him in downing them. Brett sat alone, not drinking and looking lost. I knew that Hubert wanted to join in the celebrations, because he was holding a can of lager and gazing at it with a 'should I, shouldn't I?' expression. 'I'll drive,' I mouthed to him.

Turning to Brett, I said, 'Come outside. I want to have a word with you.'

'What about?'

'The night of the accident.'

He stared at me in puzzlement. 'Are you a cop?'

'No. I'm trying to sort something out for a friend.'

Outside in the garden, we stood, backs pressed against a wall. The cold air was bracing after the stuffy atmosphere inside. Brett looked up at the sky. 'Funny how things turn out, innit? I never did like being the only one. I thought me mum was dying and now, all of a sudden, I've got a sister.'

'Your mum will need all the help she can get.'

'Yeah. I'll do my bit.'

Keen to change the subject, I said, 'Tell me about the night Trina Brampton died.'

He looked at me warily. 'I've been telling the bloody cops over and over again, but they don't believe me.'

'You tell me the truth now, Brett, and I'll

believe you.'

'I'll tell you this for a start. I'm not a frigging lunatic driver. It was a sixty-mile-an-hour limit. And I've got one of those P stickers on my car. I didn't want it to stand for prat. So I was doing sixty – give or take. It was late – after midnight – there was nothing about and then, by Finches Wood, I saw this parked car. No lights. Just as I got alongside of the car the driver's door swung open. I knew I'd hit the door – it made a right noise – but I didn't know I'd hit a woman...' He broke off.

'Is that why you didn't stop?'

'I did bloody stop. I stopped further up and looked back. I was in a panic. I thought the driver might come after me.'

'What did you see?'

'I saw a bloke leaning over someone in the road.'

'What did he look like?'

'I dunno, it was pitch dark.'

'Was he fat, thin, tall?'

He shook his head. 'I don't bloody know. If I could have described him, I bloody would have. The police think I made him up.'

'Don't get upset. You were looking back and you saw the man leaning over. Then what happened? Did you phone for an ambulance?'

'No.'

'Why not?'

'Because he did a runner and I guessed she was dead. I drove home. My stupid dad said I should report it.'

'And you did?'

'Yeah. Worst mistake I ever made. She was a cop's wife and...'

'And what?'

'They're out to get me.'

'You hadn't been drinking?'

'No. The police breathalyzed me and took blood tests.'

'Where had you been?'

'Only to see my girlfriend. The cops went to see her.'

'What for?'

'I dunno, but she told them we'd had a row and I'd stormed off.'

'She was telling the truth?'

'Yeah, but ... I'd calmed down by the time I'd got in the car. I love driving. I passed my test first time. I'm a good driver – even my dad says that.'

Shouts of, 'Brett, where are you?' from inside signalled the end of our conversation. As we went in, I said, 'I'll keep in touch and let you know if I find anything out.'

He smiled wryly. 'The pigs are flying. They'll win. There is something else I found out – her husband found the body.'

Back in the house, the doctor and midwife were leaving. 'You did a good job,' said the doctor. 'Well done.' The midwife smiled at me broadly, and as they left, more friends and neighbours arrived, carrying just about everything a baby could need. Hubert sat in an armchair looking slightly dazed. Jimmy had begun a sing-song and I was a bit concerned that mother and baby would be forgotten. I needn't have worried. Three women were seeing to Pam's needs. One was brushing Pam's hair, another was watching over the baby, who was now dressed and sleeping peacefully in a padded plastic container by Pam's bed. The third woman was tidying up. 'Here she is,' said Pam. 'The Lone Ranger. What is your name, love?'

'Kate.'

'You saved my life.'

I felt embarrassed now. I just wanted to get away. 'We're off now,' I said before she could say any more. 'Congratulations. She's a beautiful baby.'

'Yeah. You wait till I see my GP. I'm going to sue him. Stupid or what! Makes my Jimmy look like a genius. I suppose he's downstairs getting drunk?'

'He's celebrating,' I said. 'He's a happy man.'

'That's as may be. It won't last. Anyway, love, you come back and see us, and if I can ever do you a favour, I will.'

From the doorway to the living room, I nodded my head at Hubert to indicate we were leaving. Reluctantly, he got to his feet. 'I was enjoying myself,' he said.

Jimmy noticed as we tried to sidle out, and bear-hugged us both. Brett gave me a wave and Jimmy's friends waved and cheered as I drove away.

'I've never seen a baby born before,' said Hubert. 'This has been the best day of my life.'

'That's the lager talking.'

'No it isn't. I mean it. I wish I'd had kids.'

'Tell you what,' I said. 'If ever I have a baby, you'll be godfather and I'll give you full babysitting rights.'

'Do you mean that?'

'Of course I do. Now, can we change the subject and I'll tell you what Brett told me about the night Trina Brampton died.'

Twenty-One

Hubert decided, because he'd had a few drinks, that he'd stay overnight in a hotel, but first he wanted to see where I was living.

I crept up the stairs, hoping no one would see us, partly because I didn't want anyone to think Hubert was my lover, and partly because I felt physically and emotionally shattered. I didn't want to have to start talking about Victoria's murder when I'd just witnessed an unexpected birth.

Once in my room, after a quick look round and a nod of approval, Hubert sprawled on my bed. He was a little drunk – I could see that now – and he wanted to talk. 'How could Pam not know she was pregnant?' he asked.

'I've known of it before and read about it,' I said as I sat down. 'Often it's an older woman thinking she's putting on weight or being told she's in the menopause.'

'The doctor must be bloody stupid,' said Hubert, with his eyes closed.

I partly agreed with him, but occasionally patients do mislead their doctors. Once, in an outpatients department, a Chinese registrar asked a long-married woman if she could be pregnant. 'We don't have sex any more,' she'd told him haughtily. But later, in the changing room, she'd said, 'I wasn't going to tell him we only manage it once in a while. I'd rather say we'd stopped altogether.' I supposed there was some logic there, but I failed to see it.

Hubert opened his eyes and propped himself on his elbow. 'Well, am I right about the doctor? What do you think?'

'I expect she went to him,' I said, 'when the pregnancy was well advanced, and he'd made her an appointment to see a gynaecologist, presuming she had a benign tumour. In the meantime, she gave birth.'

'Strange family,' he murmured. 'Pam's blind to her pregnancy and Brett's blind to a pedestrian.'

'I had a chat with Brett, and he's quite sensible,' I said. 'It sounds as if Trina Brampton could have been pushed out of a car, or she was trying to escape from someone.'

'Her husband?'

'I think so. They'd been out together and had a row. Maybe she'd been flirting, or he thought she had, and there was a struggle and she opened the car door.'

'You're only guessing.'

'That's true, but what if Brian was guessing too, and he came to the wrong conclusion? He may have suspected Rupert was her secret lover and, still bitter and angry, he plans what he thinks is the perfect murder.'

'It sounds plausible,' said Hubert grudgingly. 'But how did they find out Brett was the hit-and-run driver?'

'He said he stopped further up the road and saw a man leaning over the body. So he drove on when he saw the man leave the scene too. He presumed then that she was dead. He was obviously in shock and he drove home. His dad persuaded him to report it to the police.'

Hubert looked thoughtful. 'All this guesswork isn't going to get you very far. And what about Victoria? Where does she fit in to all this? Don't tell me she was in the car too, and threatened to tell.'

'Hubert,' I said, with a big smile on my face. 'Sometimes you really make my day. Another person in the car is a real possibility.'

A few minutes later, Hubert fell asleep on my bed. It was ten p.m. I shrugged mentally, because I didn't have the heart to wake him now. I covered myself with my dressing gown and settled down for an uncomfortable night in a bucket chair.

Although I was tired, I couldn't sleep. At midnight my head started to nod, until a thought jolted me wide awake – *I still had the master key*. I'd had no plans to use it again but what if the police knew there was a set missing? No doubt they'd already taken away Victoria's computer and searched her office for clues, so there was little point in me taking the chance of being caught in that corridor again. But what was I going to do about the key?

Quietly I left my room and padded in bare feet towards the kitchen to make myself a hot drink. The kitchen door was not fully closed, so that a shaft of light lit the dark corridor. I hesitated for a moment but I was thirsty and chatting in the kitchen was better than fretting in an uncomfortable chair.

I couldn't hear anyone moving about in the kitchen, and even when I opened the door a fraction, I couldn't see anyone. Until, that is, I opened the door properly, and there, stepping out from behind the door, was Lorna holding a large can of evaporated milk.

'Hi, Kate,' she said cheerfully. 'How's your foot?'

'Much better, thanks.'

I paused, feeling awkward. Did she know

I'd found Victoria's body? And if she did know, should I wait for her to mention it?

'Have you heard about the burglary?' she asked.

'What burglary?'

'When the police arrived to look over Victoria's office, it had been wrecked.'

'What about the security man? Didn't he see anything?'

Lorna shook her head and swigged back the last of her evaporated milk. 'Fancy some toast?' she asked.

'Yes. Thanks. I'm hungry.'

Lorna put four thick slices of bread under the grill and stood watching them. I thought it was time to ask the question, so I said as casually as I could, 'I suppose you know I found the body?'

She didn't turn round to look at me. 'I heard you did. I didn't know you had friends in such high places.'

'She wasn't a friend. My mother knew her and I'd only met Victoria once.'

'At least they've got the bastard that did it.'

'You mean her neighbour – Dale Dutchman?'

She turned the toast over. 'That's the one.'

'I don't think he did it,' I said. 'Surely he'd have at least tried to fix up an alibi. I mean, he was bound to be first choice.'

She turned to look at me. 'Have the police interviewed you yet?'

'I still have to give a written statement.'

'They've practically lived here this week. Louise was so desperate she's had to get in agency staff.'

Now that the toast was ready, Lorna put two slices on a plate for me and began slathering butter on her own slices. Then she handed me the knife. I buttered my toast sparingly, and couldn't help watching as she attacked her toast so swiftly that the butter trickled down her chin. She really was an object lesson in the saying – *you are what you eat*.

There were two stools in the kitchen, and now I sat down to eat, but Lorna's bottom was far too large, so she had to stand. 'There's more bad news,' she said. 'Suki's given in her notice. She's going back to Thailand because her husband's very ill.'

Before I had a chance to say anything, Lorna said, 'The Thai girls never stay very long. Their contracts are meant to last a year, but some only stay three months.'

'I expect they get homesick.'

'Yeah. But I'm surprised they don't have to repay their air fare.'

'The Decker-Whites did the recruiting, didn't they?' I asked. 'So maybe they were easy-going about the contracts and their air fares.'

'Still seems odd to me.'

It did to me too, but I couldn't draw any conclusions – after all, both Decker-Whites were dead now, so who was there left to ask? One name only came to mind – the Director of Nursing – Louise Booth.

We left the kitchen at the same time, and Lorna seemed very downcast. 'I'll really miss Suki. It'll just leave you and me living in.'

That was a depressing thought, but Suki's departure was a month away, and by that time I hoped to have found out as much as I possibly could. My ambition to solve the case had diminished with the number of deaths. I had to do my best for Dale. But the question was what next?

Back in my bedroom, Hubert had vacated the bed and was now sitting in the chair half asleep. 'Your turn for the bed,' he murmured with closed eyes.

When I woke at eight a.m., Hubert had gone, and I was disappointed. I wanted to talk. He'd left me a note in bold capitals: RING ME. BE CAREFUL. TRUST NO ONE.

All very well, I thought, to give advice. I needed to take action.

I showered, dressed warmly and decided that I'd spend my last free day doing some surveillance. After all, that's what PIs are supposed to do.

I spotted Lorna going into the kitchen but she didn't see me, and as I passed her room, I noticed the door was open. I knew the kettle took a few minutes to boil, but would she be cooking any breakfast? I slipped in the door as fast as a ferret up a trouser leg. Her room was so cluttered with books and magazines and clothes strewn around the floor that it already looked 'done over'. Not knowing what I was looking for, I peered into drawers and the wardrobe, ever alert for the heavy thud of Lorna's feet. It was in the bedside table I found something that could be useful – a photograph album. I didn't want to steal it, but I reasoned I could slip it back somehow, maybe even before she realized it was missing. I slipped the album into my shoulder bag, checked the corridor was clear, and left hurriedly.

Once in my car, I allowed myself a pause and a huge sigh of relief. I couldn't have been more nervous than if I'd been shoplifting. I half expected a shout of 'Stop, thief!' but none came, and I drove off towards Finches Wood, where Trina's body had been found.

There had been no more snow but there was a cold wind, and this early on a Sunday morning, there was no one either walking or driving. It was easy to find the exact spot where Trina died – three bouquets marked the spot, flowers that had long since wilted and died. Although, on closer inspection, they might have been a mere week old. Snow and rain had obliterated the messages, but it showed that three people at least cared enough to leave flowers.

I drove further along, to where Brett might have stopped. I got out of the car and looked back, trying to imagine the scene. Perhaps I was being naïve, but even with a stormy marriage – and especially as Brian Brampton was a police officer with some first-aid training – wouldn't he have at least attempted to resuscitate his wife? Whereas, a mere friend or lover might have put other interests first – like a wife at home? Since Trina had been on the driver's side did that mean her companion had been drinking?

Dejected, because as always I had far more questions than answers, I drove on towards the village of Yardley, where Brian Brampton lived. It took me ages to find the house, partly because it was set back from the road, and partly because I didn't expect anywhere quite so grand. It was the sort of detached mock-Tudor that verged on naff, but would cost the average person at least two lifetimes of mortgage payments.

Although there were no parked cars to be seen in his leafy cul-de-sac, the drive was so long that I wasn't too worried about being seen. I parked a little to the side of the black and gold spiked gates, switched off the engine and began leafing through Lorna's photographs.

At a quick glance, I could see that, although Lorna had started off tidily, the album degenerated into hasty inserts of loose photos. I hoped none had slipped out when I left her room. I started at the beginning. Happy baby Lorna was followed by happy toddler, happy child and smiling schoolgirl. Pretty, unrecognizable, slim Lorna stared back at me until she was in her late teens. Photos of her in her student nurse's uniform showed her gaining weight. By her graduation, she was very overweight. What on earth had happened to her? Was it nursing itself, or merely stuffing herself with cheap but fattening food?

I looked up, deep in thought, to see Brian Brampton striding down his drive. I threw the album on the passenger seat, switched on the engine and drove off in a squeal of brakes.

That was a close call, I thought, as I drove out of the village. I hoped I'd been too quick for him to see my number plate. I began to relax and slow down. He probably hadn't seen my face. Stop worrying, I told myself. Until I looked in my rear-view mirror and realized the only other car on the road, a black Jaguar, was following me.

Twenty-Two

I put my foot down but the black Jag speeded up too, and my old car couldn't compete with a fast new expensive one. I drove on, and with a watchful eye on my rear-view mirror, I had to make a quick decision about which turn-off to take at the next junction. I needed to be out of the isolated rural lanes and into civilization. I took the left turn towards Little Makham. He was still right behind me, so I didn't lower my speed. What the hell was his plan anyway? Did he intend to merely drive me off the road, or force me out of the car?

Sometimes salvation comes in strange forms. Mine was a police speed trap. The man with a hand-held speed camera had clocked me doing at least sixty as I approached the village. He waved me down and I could see that the black Jag had slowed to a respectable speed. As I pulled over, he drove on past. My fear then was he'd lay in wait for me. I wound down the driver's window.

'Did you know, madam, you were doing sixty miles an hour in a forty-mile-an-hour zone?'

'Yes I did, officer.' He was exceptionally tall and not bad looking.

I noticed now that there was another officer sitting in the car. 'Would you take your time checking over the car, officer?' I said with a relieved smile. 'And do I get breathalysed now?'

'Are you being funny?' he asked, tight-lipped.

He looked over towards his colleague in the car and I saw him mouth, 'Nutter.' His partner left the warmth of the police car and ambled over. He was much shorter, older, and wore rimless glasses. 'This lady,' said the tall cop, 'wants to be breathalysed.'

'We can do that,' he said laconically. 'Any-thing else?'

'She'd like us to check over her car.'

He peered over the rimless glasses. 'We're not the AA, madam.'

'Just the tyres,' I said. 'And check my brake lights.'

'Money to burn, madam?' he asked.

'Not exactly,' I said. 'I just want to be kept here for a while.'

The pair exchanged knowing glances.

'I'm not mentally disturbed,' I snapped. 'If you must know, I was being followed.'

Even the truth didn't convince them, so I explained. 'The black Jag was following me.'

'You're sure?' asked the taller PC.

'Very sure.'

'Why didn't you tell us straight away?'

I paused. They could be friends of Brampton for all I knew. They would have heard of his wife's tragic death and be sympathetic. In the end, I blurted out, 'The man following me is a police superintendent – Brian Brampton.'

Again there was an exchange of glances. 'I never knew he had a Jag,' said Sergeant Rimless. PC Tall said, 'He's not in the force any more – he's retired.'

After telling me to stay in my car, they talked in a huddle a few yards away. I debated if I should tell them that I was working undercover. Could they keep quiet? Or would it be all round the station in less than an hour? I decided to wait and see.

Rimless was taking out a notebook, but his clipboard with the speeding tickets he put back in the police car. Then the two appeared by my side. 'Right, madam,' said Rimless. 'I've decided that you felt harassed by the black Jag and were forced to speed, so this is just a warning – obey the road signs!'

I thought that was it, but then he added, 'We'll need a few details – name, address, destination, the reason for your journey and the reason you think Mr Brampton was following you.'

'You should be in CID,' I said. I took a deep breath. 'I'm a freelance journalist,' I said. 'There's a breath of scandal about Brampton and I've been commissioned to find out all I can. I was hanging about outside his house. He saw me. I took off and he came after me.'

'More than a breath of scandal there,' said Rimless. 'More like storm force ten.'

'What do you mean? I promise I won't divulge my source.'

He smiled briefly, as if doubting anything promised by a journalist. 'It's not for me to say, is it? But how does someone on only police pay manage to live like a Premiership footballer? Ask yourself that.'

'I have, but has anyone else?'

He shrugged. 'There was an internal enquiry last year, looking at his bank account. They even searched his house. They didn't find anything. Then, when his wife got killed, there was a bit of sympathy and strangely he decided to resign. End of story as far as the police were concerned.'

'Thanks.'

'For what?'

'Just confirming that he's dodgy.'

'Don't hang around his place again,' he warned, sounding serious. 'It's rumoured he wasn't averse to hitting his wife.'

'I didn't know that. Did she have family in the area?'

'She had a sister living outside of Northampton. Name of –' he paused to think – 'Tyringham, like the health farm.'

'You're a star,' I said.

'We don't like bad apples,' he muttered. 'Gives us all a bad name.'

I was about to drive off when he said, 'We'll follow you back, and if you have any trouble, any time, get in touch. I'm Michael Dodds and my lanky friend is Paul Clark.'

As good as their word, they gave me an escort to Fair Acres. I'd had a lucky break, but I didn't plan to waste the rest of the day sitting in my room. In reception, I found a phone directory, and that quickly revealed there were only three Tyringhams in the area. I scribbled down the phone numbers and addresses and, back in my car, I began phoning. I was third time lucky, and not only was Wendy Tyringham Trina's sister – she was very willing to speak to me.

The Woods End Estate to the east of

Northampton was a large modern housing estate where all roads look the same, but there was plenty of green space and a wooded park that alleviated the sameness. Wendy's place, set in a quiet cul-de-sac, was a white chalet-style house with a neat front garden.

I'd only had a description of Trina: tall, model-thin, very attractive. Wendy too fitted that description, although she was more voluptuous. She was wearing low-cut jeans and a low-cut red jumper with ample fillage. Her long, blonde hair, pale skin and blue eyes gave her a Scandinavian appearance. She seemed pleased to see me and even offered me lunch. 'I'm on my own,' she said. 'Just soup and sandwiches. It's no trouble, and I do want to talk about Trina.'

'Sounds wonderful,' I said. 'Do you mind if I take some notes?'

'Go ahead. Just make sure you get something about my sister in the papers.'

I sat at the breakfast bar and Wendy heated home-made soup and buttered bread. 'I still can't get over it,' she said. 'Her life was fine until she met him. She was older than me – four years. That's how long she lasted married to him. He killed her. I don't know *how*, that's the trouble.'

'What makes you think that?'

'I haven't got any evidence, if that's what you mean, but I do know she was frightened of him.'

'He was violent?'

'She'd deny it. That was her way. All her life she'd kept an eye out for me, and when our mum died, we bought this house together.'

'She was nursing then?'

'Yes. At the General. But she did a little modelling on the side. She was happy. Then she met Brampton one night when she was working in A&E. She was thirty-three, he was more than ten years older and divorced.'

'You didn't approve?'

Wendy didn't answer but went to the fridge and stared inside. She withdrew a packet of cheese, and then with a sharp knife began cutting ultra-thin slices. When she'd finished, she turned to me, the knife still in her hand. 'If I met him and I had some sort of weapon with me –' she paused – 'I'd kill him.'

'Did your sister love him?'

She put down the knife. 'At first she did, but gradually she changed. I saw bruises on her arms and legs. She always made up excuses, usually saying it had happened at work.'

'Do you think Brampton loved her?'

'He wanted to possess her. He was always

224

phoning her, even at work, and Trina told me sometimes she'd seen him waiting for her in the car park, and then he'd follow her car home.'

'What do you think happened the night she died?'

Wendy turned away from me and began carefully arranging the cheese on the bread. I stared at my notebook. I was drawing the car and the open driver's door.

When the sandwiches were ready, she plated them and began ladling out the soup. Finally she muttered miserably, 'I wish I knew what had happened. The police version is that a boy called Brett Yule was speeding and his car hit her.'

'He has admitted it,' I said.

'Yes, and that's one of the reasons the police only concentrated on him. Open and shut case, according to them. No real investigation.'

'You think there was someone else in the car with her?'

She nodded. 'Yes, but I don't know who.'

'Could it have been another man?'

'I suppose so,' she admitted reluctantly. 'Trina had lots of admirers, but she wouldn't have been unfaithful. She wouldn't. She had standards.'

We began eating the soup and fell silent. It

had become obvious that Wendy didn't want her sister's memory tarnished by any suggestion that she'd been carrying on an affair. After a while, I changed tack slightly. 'Brett the so-called hit-and-run driver told me he stopped further on and saw a man leaning over the body. He guessed your sister was dead because the man then ran away.'

Wendy looked up from her soup bowl. 'Strange, isn't it, that Brampton told the police he hadn't realized Trina hadn't come home until he woke at five a.m.? Her body had lain on that road for hours. If she worked a late shift – which wasn't that often – it was from five p.m. to twelve midnight in the operating theatre. Trina told me once that Brian always waited up for her. He didn't need to wait up for her, did he? He knew she was already dead.'

'According to the only witness,' I said, 'that is, the driver who actually caused your sister's death, it was unavoidable – she opened the car door and got out just as he approached.'

'That says it all, doesn't it? She was scared for her life. The only way she could escape from him was to scramble out of the car.'

Over the cheese sandwiches, I thought about the chances of convicting Brampton of any charge relating to his wife's death.

Even if his colleagues had suspicions that he was with her in the car that night, frightening his wife into jumping out of her car would be impossible to prove. Case dismissed. Not proven.

'There is another possibility, Wendy,' I said slowly. She looked up eagerly.

'Your sister went to meet someone in the woods. After all, she had stopped for a reason. The person she was expecting didn't turn up and someone else got into the passenger seat. Someone she feared even more than her husband.'

Twenty-Three

Wendy stared at me long and hard. 'I *want* it to be him. I want him to go to prison for harming my sister.'

'If she didn't report his violence—' I began.

'You still don't understand, do you?' she said.

'Understand what?'

'I told you my sister had standards. Well, she did. And she was going to blow the whistle on the goings-on at Fair Acres.'

'What goings-on?'

Wendy's face showed her disappointment that I too didn't know the facts. 'I'm not sure,' she said. 'Trina wouldn't tell me any details. She said if I knew I'd be in danger.'

'From Brian?'

Again Wendy was uncertain. 'I don't know.' Her eyes filled with tears. 'I only have suspicions, but I do know that Brian was wary of Rupert Decker-White.'

'In what way?'

'Trina told me once that Rupert was a

powerful man.'

'Did she find him attractive?'

'Yes, I think she did,' she murmured.

'So Brian might have been jealous?'

'Trina wasn't having an affair with him, if that's what you're trying to imply,' she snapped. 'Don't you write anything like that.'

'I just want to find out the truth,' I said. 'My job is on the line.'

'And my sister's reputation and memory matter more to me than your poxy job.'

Wendy's face had reddened and she was obviously getting upset.

'If Brian is the suspicious, possessive type,' I said, 'and it sounds as if he is, he might have thought your sister was having an affair. That could be a motive, but why Victoria?'

'But I thought ... I heard that a man had been arrested for the murder of Victoria.'

'I think he's innocent.'

Wendy rested her chin on her hand and stared ahead. 'He'll get away with it, won't he? He'll do a runner. He'll go off to Thailand again.'

'What do you mean, *again*?'

'He went over there three times a year at least. He loved it there.'

'With Trina?'

'She went once a year, but she wasn't so keen.'

'Why not?'

There was no answer. Wendy looked uncomfortable. 'Trina told me he went out on his own when they were there. She thought he was looking for young girls.'

'He really is a charmer, isn't he?' I said. 'Don't worry, he won't get away with it.'

'He has so far,' she said bitterly.

Wendy stood up then, and began filling the kettle. 'When Trina went to Thailand,' she said over the noise of the running water, 'they all went together.'

'You mean with the Decker-Whites?'

'Yes,' she murmured. 'Rupert recruited staff there.'

'That puzzles me,' I said.

'Why?'

'I just wondered why the director of nursing – Louise Booth – didn't go headhunting. After all, she would be more likely to be able to choose the best candidates.'

'I don't know about nursing,' said Wendy. 'I work in a building society.'

She made tea and we drank it in silence. 'You'll let me see the article before it's published?' she asked as I was about to leave.

'Of course,' I said with a smile. Inwardly I cringed. Once, I'd found lying difficult, now it was mere role play.

Wendy waved me goodbye and I intended

to go straight back to Fair Acres, but at the sight of Lorna's photo album that I'd 'borrowed', I drove around the corner, stopped and began a belated close look at Lorna's photos. I flicked quickly through those I'd already seen, when one in particular caught my eye: one of a young Lorna, eighteen or so, in uniform at a party – judging by the decorations, a Christmas party. She'd begun to fill out, and with full breasts and a shapely waist, she was stunning. A tall handsome man in a white coat stood with his arm around her. I looked closely at the medic and I was as sure as I could be that the man was none other than Rupert Decker-White. Hurriedly, I checked for more photos of them together, but there were none.

She had, though, kept a faithful record of hospital events – Christmas, Easter, summer barbecues and parties. There were no more photos of Lorna, slim or fat. She became simply an observer. The photographs of Fair Acre parties were interesting. They weren't exactly orgies but they did seem wild and drunken affairs. In some photos, people lay on the floor, obviously too drunk to stand; men and women in various states of undress posed and paraded around making an eighteen-to-thirty holiday look quite tame. Had Lorna deliberately focused on the more riotous aspects, or was this how it was? In one photo, Brian was in a clinch with Polly, in another Rupert was clutching the breasts of Louise Booth, whilst Victoria was caught on camera passionately kissing another woman whose face I couldn't see. I needed time to look at them properly, but I also needed to put the album back before it was missed. Lorna's photos weren't of the best quality, but at least I now knew how Rupert had died virtually unnoticed by so many.

Back at Fair Acres, a note had been slipped under my door. Louise hoped my foot was better, and could I collect theatre garb and mules from Doris at eight thirty a.m. for a nine a.m. to six p.m. shift in the theatre's packing and sterilizing area.

I heard voices along the corridor and guessed Lorna and Suki were on their way to the kitchen. I crept out and my luck was in, for Lorna's door was open. I took the album from my shoulder bag and sneaked into her room and slipped it back into the drawer of her bedside table. I was just at the door as Lorna approached. It looked suspicious but I smiled and said, 'Hi. I was just looking for you. I'm in theatre tomorrow – general dogs-body, I think, but mainly doing the instrument packs. I'm a bit nervous – I wondered if you'd got any tips.'

Her eyes seemed to narrow in her large face. Perhaps I'd said too much, perhaps I sounded nervous. 'How's your foot?' she asked.

'Good as new,' I said.

'Suki's just made some tea,' said Lorna, smiling. 'We're having it here. Come and join us.'

I trooped back into Lorna's room and moments later Suki appeared with a tray of tea, chocolate biscuits and cake. I wanted to ask about any developments with Victoria's murder, but Lorna was too busy gorging on chocolate biscuits. Suki looked away rather than watch Lorna eat. I began to feel like a voyeur, so I said directly to Suki, 'Have the police been here again?'

'Oh yes,' she said. 'There are rumours the fraud squad are involved, and we may be closed down.'

'I'm sure it won't come to that,' I said, trying to reassure her, but I wasn't sure at all. A private hospital loses its reputation and customers will go elsewhere.

'You're planning to go home anyway,' snapped Lorna to Suki.

'Yes, but I heard today my husband is a little better, so I may be coming back.'

With her mouth full of chocolate biscuit, Lorna said, 'But you won't be coming back

233

here – will you?'

Suki thought for a moment. 'I'd like to work by the sea. I haven't seen the sea here.'

'If you do that,' said Lorna. 'I'll follow you.'

Suki's expression, usually calm and equable, changed, and I realized for the first time that she didn't actually like Lorna. I supposed it was a relationship born of loneliness and necessity.

Between the biscuits and the cake, Lorna explained my duties in theatre, which included disposal of waste, washing of instruments and equipment, and then putting together the operation packs ready for sterilization. Thankfully, a technician organized the actual sterilization.

'You have to be meticulous,' she said. 'Fair Acres is fairly well equipped, but it doesn't compare with the NHS. The loss of a scalpel or a pair of scissors is a major catastrophe.' Then she laughed. 'Don't look so worried, Kate. Everything is checked and double-checked according to a big folder of diagrams. And you won't be working alone.'

As I made my exit, I noticed Suki's sad expression and wondered if she was going back to Thailand partly to escape from Lorna. Her words, 'I'll follow you', seemed likely to be borne out, unless it was mere coincidence that Lorna and Rupert had landed up in the same place. If she'd deliberately followed him, was it for his surgical skills or was she a stalker? Was she obsessed with the idea that her *only* hope of losing weight was surgical intervention, and that, as he'd offered his services for free, it was an offer she couldn't refuse. If, however, she was a stalker, she'd been a very low-key one, but fear of losing her job and her accommodation might have curbed her being too obvious.

Back in my room, I couldn't relax. Scenarios and possibilities and maybes and perhaps this and perhaps that distorted my thinking. All I knew for certain was that Brian Brampton had a history of violence, and that Dale Dutchman was being questioned for Victoria's murder.

I decided to have a long hot bath and think calming thoughts. It worked, for I very nearly fell asleep in the bath.

Later, as I dozed watching TV in bed, David rang. I told him about my visit to Trina's sister and her view that there were 'goings-on' at Fair Acres that seemed sinister.

'I think you should give your witness account to the police tomorrow,' he said coldly. 'And then pack your bags. I'll collect you.'

'Why?' I demanded.

'I can't tell you any more. But this is bigger than you think.'

'Good,' I said. 'Cracking a big case has more job satisfaction than catching errant husbands. So I'm staying put.'

'I don't want you there. It's not safe. If someone gets the impression that the police are closing in, valuable evidence could be lost.'

'I want a few more days.'

'No.'

'What are you going to do, carry me out kicking and screaming?'

'Don't push me. Or I'll bring some of the lads along.'

I paused, realizing he could do just that. 'All I'm asking,' I said quietly, trying to keep calm, 'is a few more days. I could be on the verge of a breakthrough.'

'You've found out something?' he asked in a more reasonable tone.

'I've found out all sorts of stuff,' I said. 'But it's like a jigsaw and I need a few more pieces for it to reveal itself.'

'So, you haven't got half a picture yet?'

'You're beginning to sound like Hubert.'

'Maybe I am, but I want to marry you, not see you buried.'

'Please, David, I start in theatre tomorrow. By the end of the week I'll give up. OK?'

He sighed. 'OK. Phone me twice a day. Tell me where you are and be prepared to leave at very short notice.'

I finally realized what he was hinting at. The police were going to raid Fair Acres.

Twenty-Four

Hubert phoned directly after David. He was still thrilled by his childbirth experience. So thrilled he wondered if he was too old to become a midwife.

'Yes,' I told him bluntly.

He changed the subject then to his night in the hotel, and how one of the drivers had stayed overnight to care for Jasper. Jasper had been 'offish' with him for an hour or two after his return, but was now back to normal. I waited for him to mention my fairly imminent return, as I guessed David and he were colluding in getting me off the case.

'How's Shirley-Marie?' I asked out of politeness.

'She's splendid,' he said. 'She's planning a surprise for me.'

I hoped it wasn't a surprise visit. Where would I go if she arrived within days? I certainly couldn't cope with a quasi *ménage à trois*. I could of course move into a B&B. I didn't say any of this to Hubert.

'Has David been in touch?' he asked, trying to sound casual.

'You know damn well he has,' I said. 'I'm staying, at least until the end of the week.'

'I told him you'd be stroppy.'

'I'm not being stroppy. I'm trying to be professional. I start a case and I want to see it through.'

'Even though your client is dead?'

'More so.'

'I knew I'd be wasting my time,' he muttered.

'You are. I'll be careful.'

'That'll make a change.'

'I'll keep in touch,' I said.

He muttered something unintelligible as he hung up. Suddenly I felt very weary and dispirited. What the hell was I going to do next? David seemed to be implying the police were going to make a move, but against whom? Was I being blind? Had I failed already?

The next morning at eight thirty I was trying the handle of Doris's little empire. It was locked but I could hear her moving about inside. I called her name loudly three times, and eventually she answered the door. I could see immediately that there was something wrong. Her thin lips had a bluish tinge and her face was tight and drawn.

'Are you ill?' I asked. 'Shall I fetch a doctor?'

'No *thank* you,' she said firmly. 'I'm just having one of my turns. I get a bit of angina, that's all. Now, what do you want? Not too fat for those uniforms already, are you?'

'No,' I said sharply, hoping she'd get the message that I didn't need any lectures on my weight. 'I need some theatre gear. I'm working in the sterilizing department.'

'Sit down then. What size clogs?'

'Six.'

She raised her eyebrows. 'You wait here,' she said. 'I've just remembered I haven't renewed my angina patch.' She ferreted around in her shopping bag, found her patch and then disappeared into a back room. The shopping bag sat next to her sewing machine and I couldn't resist a quick peek. Even without rooting around, I could see she had a virtual chemist's shelf in the bag. There was warfarin and glycerol trinitrate, ranitidine, allergy tablets and ibuprofen. There were also small unmarked boxes with the handwritten words – *Slimming Pills*. Unfortunately, I didn't hear her approaching. 'You're a nosy bitch,' she said.

'Your bag slipped,' I said. 'I think I've picked up everything that fell out.'

'I bet someone told you I've got slimming pills,' she said. 'Fat Lorna won't take them, but she likes being fat.'

'Do they work?' I asked.

'They worked for Trina Brampton, not that she needed more than a week's supply. And that Aussie girl – Polly. She takes them.'

'How much?' I asked.

'To you, a week's supply, twenty quid.'

I hesitated, but not for long. 'I'll try them. They are safe, I suppose?'

'Of course they are. But don't blab about them. Come down for them later. I leave the door open in the afternoons – the security man locks up for me at about nine. You'll find the pills in there.' She nodded her head towards a back room. There's a cupboard with some old bales of material in it. You'll find a packet with your name on it at the back of a bale of blue striped cotton. Take one first thing in the morning and one between two and three.'

'What do they contain?'

'I don't ask,' she said sharply, 'because I don't want to know. It's black-market stuff, so don't be too picky.'

'You mean they're illegal?'

'Of course they are. Take my advice, love. Lose some weight and don't breathe a word about the tablets. You don't want to get on the wrong side of the law, do you?'

'No, of course not,' I said. Suddenly I seemed to be in the wrong, and dotty Doris a mere supplier of a dream of effortless slimness. I knew many slimming pills had been banned over the years. Some worked and occasionally I did wonder if they had been removed from circulation simply because they *did* work. After all, a multi-million-pound slimming industry would grind to a halt if there was a safe magic pill.

As I was leaving with two white trouser suits and a pair of white clogs, Doris held out her hand for her twenty pounds. I managed to gather together nineteen pounds in coins and notes, leaving me with no money for lunch in the staff restaurant. 'Leave the pound coin you owe me where you find your tablets,' said Doris with a sly smile. I turned to go. 'Stay there a minute,' she said, walking over to the sink, where she half filled a mug with water. Then, from her shopping bag, she opened a small white box and removed two tablets.

'There you are, dear,' she said, opening her tiny fist. 'A sample for you. Save you bothering with lunch.'

I felt I didn't have much option, and secretly I wanted to try them. I'd led a drug-free existence until now. I'd never tried ecstasy, never smoked a spliff. This was in a good cause, I told myself. I swallowed the tablet with the water and left Doris, feeling weirdly optimistic, as if after a week on slimming pills I would be transformed into a svelte size ten.

In theatre, the first hour was spent inducting me into the mysteries of the sanctum. I was led around masked and gowned. I was shown how to scrub up, because even the packing of unsterile instruments had to be as clean as possible. There was only one problem – I was flying high. My mind and body felt revitalized, even reinvented. I wanted to talk and sing and laugh. I felt ultra-alert and very happy. It was better than being in love. I didn't fear anything. No wonder slimming pills were banned, I thought. Slimmers would be the happiest people in the world. Although I'd guessed that my 'happy' pill was an amphetamine, I didn't care.

My partner in packing was a forty-something single mum called Venus. I guessed she was over forty, because she told me her eldest child was twenty-one. The youngest was six and there were two others. She had perfect unlined skin and a wide smile.

'Their father only returns for stud duties,' she told me in a lilting Barbadian accent as we sat at our station sorting instruments 'He gets in the way. Him just another mouth to feed, but he makes lovely babies.'

Later, during our coffee, Venus offered me home-made ginger cake, but I didn't need food. My mouth was dry but my appetite had disappeared, and at that moment I felt I could conquer the world.

A message from the theatre manager, to say the police wanted to see me in reception, slightly dulled my optimism, but the sooner my witness statement was given the better. I changed into my normal uniform dress and almost skipped down to reception. A granite-faced woman in a grey suit intro-duced herself as DS Colette French and told me she was accompanied by DI Jack Leyland. He was overweight, silent and un-smiling.

'We'll take your statement at the station if that's all right with you?' said DS French.

'Fine,' I said. 'Gets me off work.'

In the car, they ignored me for some time while they complained about everything from unpaid overtime to 'piss poor' canteen meals. I sat in the back seat tapping my feet up and down. I couldn't keep still.

After about five miles, DI Leyland said, 'We know who you are.'

I giggled. 'I suppose you know where I live

as well?'

'Are you on something?' French demanded.

'Me? Of course not. If you know who I am, you know what I'm doing at Fair Acres.'

'We know, but others don't,' said Leyland. 'No one likes amateurs. You should be in the real world.'

'Look, mate,' I said. 'Finding a body in a mega fridge was real enough for me. She was my client.'

'Fair point, I suppose,' said Leyland, 'but we're closing in and closing down Fair Acres, so your job is over.'

'May I ask why you're closing it down?'

They both answered no in unison.

'Could I ask when this will happen?'

'We've told the admissions manager to stop all new admissions for the time being,' said French.

'What about the staff?' I asked, thinking of Suki and Lorna being made homeless at short notice.

'Might just be temporary,' said Leyland. 'Some will be reinstated. Depends what the staff have been up to.'

'What do you think they've been up to?'

'You're a PI – you should know.'

'If I did know, I'd have done something about it.'

'Really? We take a broader view. We want the main players.'

'Bully for you,' I muttered under my breath.

In the interview room, I was asked a few standard questions and then asked to write my version of events. As I wrote, my mind raced but my fingers couldn't keep up and consequently my handwriting was a scrawled mess. Describing the finding of the body I found particularly difficult, because it re-opened the memory of the horrific sight of poor Victoria's face. I found my right hand trembling and I had to put the pen down for a few seconds.

When I'd finished, even I could hardly read it. Leyland read it through frowning, but said it could be typed up later and kept with the original. I signed it, added the date, and they both signed it. Then I was told I was free to go.

I was driven back to Fair Acres by a young PC who talked about football in a dull monotone. Even a lively exposition would have made no difference. I was bored rigid by football, but physically I couldn't keep still. Obviously my slimming pill worked on the premise that constant fidgeting used up calories.

It was one o'clock when I arrived back, and

I met Polly on her way to lunch. 'Come with me,' she said. 'I've got a bit of goss.' How could I refuse?

The array of food made me feel nauseous, so I opted for orange juice.

'You on the happy pills?' she asked.

I nodded.

'Be careful,' she said. 'You know they're not kosher.'

'What do you mean?'

'They get sold for all sorts of reasons – slimming, staying awake, phobic states, anxiety.'

'What are they then?'

'Methamphetamines. Made in Burma. Available in Thailand.'

'Addictive?' I asked, quite unnecessarily, because already I was looking forward to my next one.

'If you've got a supply, Kate – get rid. The police know. They want the real dealers, but they'll target users to get more info.'

We'd sat at a table for two, and I sipped my orange juice as dreams of size-ten clothes slipped away.

'Have you heard about Marie O'Grady?' asked Polly.

'No. What about her?'

'She's been arrested.'

'What for?'

'No one knows,' said Polly. 'But it could be for Rupert's murder.'

Before I could ask more, Polly said, 'It's my birthday on Wednesday. I'm having a party. I know it might seem a bit tasteless at the moment, but this could be the end for Fair Acres, and I feel like one last bash. Everyone's invited, the more the merrier.'

'Great. You having it here?'

She shook her head. 'No, we're having it at Brian's place – plenty of room there.'

'You mean ex-Superintendent Brian Brampton?'

'The same. We've been having a bit of a fling. He's a very sexy guy.'

One thought went through my mind. He'd recognize me. Maybe he even knew what I was doing at Fair Acres. I could be walking into a trap. But I wasn't important enough to worry him. Or was I?

Twenty-Five

After my unofficial lunch break with no lunch included, I returned to the theatre suite and Venus. She'd begun an inventory and general clean-up, but she looked miserable.

'We can go at four,' she said. 'Tomorrow we just clean. The rumour is we'll be paid until the end of the month and then ... nothing.'

'What will you do?' I asked.

'Agency work. I've done it before. What about you?' she asked.

'I'll do the same.'

I told her about the party, but she didn't seem interested. 'I'll probably go,' I said.

'I went to the New Year party,' she said, 'but I left early. Everyone was drunk by ten. I enjoy myself but I don't drink.'

'That was the night Rupert Decker-White died, wasn't it?'

Venus nodded. 'I knew something was going to happen that night. I just knew it.'

'Why was that?'

She shrugged. 'People were very drunk, getting nasty, some of them.'

I smiled. 'Fascinating,' I said. 'I like a bit of drama.'

She gave me a sharp look. 'Brian came in late, and Rupert wasn't pleased to see him. He was mad. They started arguing and they walked off together. I couldn't hear what they were saying. A bit later, I saw the food was running low, and we knew there was more laid out in the kitchen, so I went to get some more. I heard Brian shouting, saying it was too risky, and Rupert asking, "What the hell has changed?" Then Brian said, "My wife is dead because of you." Then I walked in and they both walked out.'

'What did the police say?'

Venus stared at me. 'I didn't tell the police.'

'Why not?'

'If you were a black woman, you'd know.'

'You mean they're racist?'

'Some are, but they protect their own, don't they? I didn't want to get involved.'

'What did you think about Rupert?'

'He was like a lot of men,' she said. 'He couldn't keep his trousers up.'

'Did Victoria know?'

Venus thought for a moment. 'She tried not to show it. I think a woman knows. I always knew when my man cheated on me.'

We were interrupted then by a knock at the door and the technician cheerfully announcing a meeting at four p.m. in the restaurant. 'Everyone free should be there, otherwise Louise will lose her rag.'

Venus raised her eyebrows. 'I'll make some coffee. No point in any more work.'

At four p.m. we massed in the restaurant. There were faces I'd never seen before, and a few familiar ones. I scanned the tables. Mark Alba and Polly sat together. Alice sat with Julie and Beryl, whilst Lorna and Suki sat alone. Rav sat with the other medics and everyone looked up when Marie O'Grady appeared and, looking nervously around the room, decided to sit with me and Venus. I was longing to ask her about her 'arrest', but at that moment Louise Booth made her entrance. She looked as if she'd been crying, and although the mood wasn't ugly, there was a hint that it might become so. 'We've got mortgages to pay,' shouted a male voice. 'What's going on?' shouted another. Louise stood on a chair and a sudden hush fell, as if she were going to produce the Ten Commandments. 'There is nothing I can do,' she began. 'But try to ensure that everyone is paid a month's redundancy money. Fair Acres will close on Monday. It's tragic for us all, but I'll do everything I can to ensure you get jobs elsewhere.'

There was no more shouting, just an eerie silence as they waited for Louise to say more. Except that she didn't. She stepped down from the chair, shrugged off people who wanted to talk to her, and rushed out.

'Well,' said Venus. 'Wasn't worth us coming, was it?'

I agreed it wasn't. 'I'm going home,' she said. 'I've got to find a new job.'

Marie sat staring into space, not bothering to say goodbye to Venus. 'What will I do,' she murmured. It wasn't a question because she saw no answer. It was just a sad statement of a life changed, a job lost and her security and certainty taken away.

'How will you manage for money?' I asked, knowing that at her age and with her mental health problems, another nursing post might be hard to find.

'Money isn't a problem,' she said dully. 'Being alone is.'

I fetched us coffee from the machine, and when we'd sat silently for several minutes, I said cautiously, 'I heard the police interviewed you.'

She nodded but said nothing.

'Was it about Rupert?'

There was a long pause before she said,

'Yes, but it was mostly about Victoria. Where was I on the day? Et cetera. I told them nowadays I had trouble lifting my shopping, never mind heaving a body into a fridge.'

'What did they say to that?'

'Weren't nurses meant to be strong and able to lift patients? I told them I could once, but now that I was a ward manager, others did the lifting.'

'Why should they suspect you anyway?'

She managed a half smile. 'I wasn't always in my fifties, neurotic and invisible. I knew Rupert years back. I met him when I was in my twenties. I was never that gorgeous, but we worked together on a cruise ship and we ... got close. One night, during a storm, a passenger was taken ill with violent abdominal pains. I tried to persuade him not to operate, but he seemed to want the drama and he was convinced that the patient had a perforated peptic ulcer.'

'What happened?'

'She died on the table. He botched it totally. She had an inflamed gall bladder. He removed that, cut through a blood vessel and she bled to death. He told the woman's husband she'd had a bad reaction to the anaesthetic.'

'Was there a post-mortem?'

'No. The husband gave his permission for

253

her to be buried at sea. But there was an inquiry later. I gave evidence and, God forgive, I lied through my teeth.'

'What about the anaesthetist?'

'He was a doctor. I don't know if he was a qualified anaesthetist. He lied too.'

'It doesn't explain,' I said, 'why the police should think you had anything to do with Victoria's death?'

Marie paused. 'I admitted to them I'd sent Rupert postcards with "ONE DAY" written on them.'

'Why did you do that?'

Marie shrugged. 'I suppose I wanted him to know that one day we'd all be called to account for that woman's death – either in this life or the next.'

'Why, though, would you want to harm Victoria?'

'I don't know why they suspected me, but I think I convinced them I had nothing to do with either death.'

She began rubbing her hands together nervously. 'I've spent my life regretting that woman's death. I've tried to be a good nurse, but ... I'm a failure.'

'Why do you say that?'

'I didn't tell you the crux of the matter. The day of that operation at sea ... we'd all been drinking. And I've admitted to the police that for some time now I've been stealing sleeping tablets and using drugs – Doris's "slimming" pills.'

'Doris has a lot to answer for,' I said.

'She's been arrested.'

'Good.'

Marie's eyes had filled with tears.

'You have to forgive yourself, Marie,' I said. 'Think of the people you've helped over the years.'

'I suppose so,' she agreed reluctantly. 'At least I didn't kill anyone deliberately.'

I was on my way back to my room when I literally bumped into Rav. He looked downcast. 'Depressing news, isn't it?' I said.

He merely nodded.

'What will you do?' I asked.

'I'll find a job somewhere,' he said. 'I might try Australia.'

'But you're getting married next year.'

He gave a slight shrug and it was obvious that he wanted to get away from me as fast as possible. 'Are you going to Polly's party?' I asked, not willing to let him go quite so easily.

'Why not?' he said, as he walked away. 'See you there.'

In my corridor, the kitchen lights were on and Suki appeared with a tray of tea, heading for Lorna's room. She pretended not to see me, and I pretended not to see her as I slipped into my room and stood staring aimlessly at a darkening sky. Working undercover hadn't worked for me. The whole thing had been a fiasco and I'd been afraid that my cover would be broken; it seemed ironic now that three weeks later the hospital was being shut down. It wasn't my fault, but somehow I felt I'd had a hand in it.

I sat on the bed and began doodling in my notebook. Three deaths marked by crosses. Two that *could* have been accidental, and at the time the police may have thought they were accidents too – until Victoria died. What did the two dead women have in common?

The impression I'd been given about Trina was that she was an airhead interested only in fashion and maintaining her looks. But, according to her sister Wendy, she had standards and she was the responsible type. Victoria seemed a different, more serious person, prone to drinking too much, but maybe that was due to her bereavement. She dealt with figures. She was logical and honest. She could have kept quiet about the extra money she'd discovered belonging to her husband, but she didn't. She blew the whistle. They were both whistleblowers. And

someone was very afraid they would be discovered.

What about Rupert? I asked myself.
Someone had offered him poison, popped it
into his mouth with a smile – either a very
close male friend or a woman. My bet was
on a woman. Who and why, I didn't know.
But I guessed it was something very personal
and not planned. One peanut in a host of
prunes seemed a lottery.

I was still deep in thought when my mobile
rang. It was Hubert.

'Great news, Kate,' he said excitedly. 'Shirley-Marie's on her way over. She'll be here
tomorrow.'

I ground out the word: 'Wonderful.'

He talked on cheerfully, told me Jasper was
fine and that he was busy, but he would get
a locum director in for a week, so that he
could spend time with Shirley-Marie.

I couldn't bear much more, so I said,
'Must go. I can hear someone crying.'

As I ended the call, the tears came.

Twenty-Six

Having hardly slept, I was tempted the next morning to take my remaining 'slimming' pill. I stared at it in my hand and knew I wanted that hyper-alert feeling, the feeling that I could conquer the world. I clutched the pill for several minutes and, although I decided not to take it, I couldn't bring my- self to throw it away.

A knock at my door at seven fifteen was Lorna bearing a message. I wasn't needed in theatre, and Louise would like to see me at eight thirty. I was a little concerned by the fact that the nursing boss wanted to see me. Had I been sussed? Was my undercover foray at an end? Lorna peered at me through puffy eyes. 'You all right?' she asked.

'I'm fine, just wondering why Louise wants to see me.'

'Just about a reallocation until Monday, I expect.' Then she added, 'We move out on Sunday. Suki's flying out Monday morning.'

'What will you do?'

'I'm going with her.'

My first reaction was sympathy for Suki.

'I'll help her look after her husband,' said Lorna. 'She can get work in Bangkok and I'll do my bit in the house.'

'It could work for you both,' I said. 'Best of luck.' She'd half turned to go when I said, 'What about the police?'

'What about them?'

'Aren't they still questioning people about Victoria's death?'

'Yeah. They're checking out alibis. Suki and I were here, so we're OK.'

'Oh,' I said. 'That's good.'

As she walked away, I wondered idly why Lorna didn't seem a tad surprised to be considered suspect enough to need an alibi. What reason could either of them have for killing Victoria? I didn't dwell long on the problem; I showered, washed my hair and made myself a breakfast of tea and toast.

At exactly eight thirty a.m. I stood outside Louise Booth's office and knocked twice.

It seemed an age before she answered, but when she did, she managed a smile and a 'Come on in and sit down'. I felt her smile was false, but she looked immaculate in a black suit and red blouse, although her eyes had a haunted expression. The desk drawers were on the floor and she was obviously packing and sorting. 'The police have given me permission,' she said, indicating the clutter with a nod of her head. 'They've already been through all my paperwork. I don't know what they were expecting to find.' For a few moments, she rearranged some papers on her desk, as if forgetting I was there. Then she looked up at me and said, 'I'm giving some staff the option of leaving straight away. My qualified staff will stay until Monday, but if you wish to leave today, please do so. You will be paid, of course. Victoria managed the payroll with some part-time help, and they'll do their best to pay everyone as quickly as possible.'

'I'll leave on Sunday if that's all right.'

'That's fine. You can either work on Washington or Churchill. Please yourself.'

'Have you got anything planned?' I asked.

She gave a brief laugh. 'My plans always seem to go wrong, so I've decided to go with the flow.'

'Are you going to Polly's party on Saturday?' I asked.

'It's a farewell bash now, isn't it? Yes, why not? You going?'

I nodded.

'See you there,' she said as I left her office.

Just as I was approaching Washington Ward,

Rav was leaving. He walked past me, eyes focused straight ahead, with no flicker of recognition.

I found Mark at the nurse's station, looking distracted.

'I've never been in a situation like this before. One minute I'm being told to clear the rooms, the next I'm being told to leave the ward ready to open up at a moment's notice. It seems there's an Aussie company interested in buying it if they can start up fairly soon.'

'How soon is soon?' I asked.

'Couple of months, I think.'

'So, they could re-employ everyone?'

'It's possible,' he said.

I was directed to work with Alice, who I eventually found drinking tea on her own in the ward kitchen. 'I'll be glad to get out of this bloody place,' she said. 'As for our mincing manager – he makes me sick.'

'Are you sure that's not vitriol you're drinking?' I said.

'You trying to be funny? You've only worked here for five minutes. You know nothing about this place.'

'What's Mark done to upset you?' I asked as I made myself a cup of tea.

She shrugged. 'I can't stand gays, as you know, but he's making a big mistake this time. I've seen his boyfriends come and go, but this time he's asking for trouble.'

'Who are you talking about?'

She began rinsing her tea cup with her back to me and muttered, 'That Rav Singh – whatever his name is.'

'I thought he was straight,' I said.

'He'd like to be, that's the problem. That's why he's planning to get married. His family will go ballistic if they find out he's gay.'

'Did Mark tell you that?'

'Yeah. I told him, I said, you be careful or you'll get bumped off. He said *he* wasn't in any danger, but Rav's family would be shamed and they might kill him. But if he married he'd be safe.'

'That sounds a bit dramatic.'

'That's all we get here – death and drama.'

For once I agreed with Alice.

We left the kitchen and began our 'round' of the three remaining patients, who were all due for discharge. They'd had breakfast and were dressed and ready to go. We moved on then to the empty rooms. 'We've got to strip all the beds,' said Alice, 'even if they're made up. Mark has decided on a spring clean. He wants a job here when it reopens, so he wants it all perfect. Gays are like that, aren't they?'

'How do you mean?'

'Pernickety.'

Alice needed no prompting to talk. As we stripped beds and disinfected lockers, she kept up a running commentary.

'This place is jinxed,' she said as she wiped over the window sill. 'Ever since Trina died. I suppose it was an accident, but it was convenient, wasn't it? A bit like Princess Di's so-called accident. Then that Rupert died – stupid name. That was no accident, but how could the police prove it? After that, there was the lady Victoria – stuck up bitch, she was. I bet whoever murdered her didn't think she'd be found for a while.'

'What do you mean?' I asked.

She flashed me a sly glance and then stared out of the window. 'You found her, didn't you?'

'Yes, I did.'

'Bit of a shock, that?' she said.

'A really big shock.'

'No blood round the fridge, was there?' she queried.

'How could you know that?'

'Stands to reason – if you'd seen blood you wouldn't have been so shocked.'

Alice was as sharp as a Stanley knife.

'I bet you read true-crime books, Alice.'

''Course I do. Great they are. Can't stand romances. Love will always let you down.'

263

'So you think whoever murdered Victoria was going to come back for the body and dispose of it some other way?'

'Makes sense to me,' she said. 'Pack a few clothes in a suitcase and make out she'd gone away. You turned up and spoiled the plans.'

'Why bother to put her in the fridge?'

'Cool the body so that the time of death couldn't be established, or just to make the place look tidy. The fridge might not have been opened for a couple of days.'

I watched as Alice continued working. Why the hell hadn't this occurred to me? I was supposed to be the professional, and there was Alice with her prejudiced mind, managing to come up with an angle I hadn't thought of.

'OK, Alice,' I said. 'I give up. Who did it?'

She gave a little harsh laugh. 'I'm not that clever, but Victoria was a woman who wore blinkers. She knew her husband was no angel. Those trips to Thailand – you can bet he was up to something there.'

'What's your guess on that one?'

'I know what he was doing.'

'What was he doing?'

'He was drug running, of course.'

'You mean Doris's slimming pills?'

'That's a laugh. The mad old bat will get

away with dealing the stuff, because she acts all innocent. She knew what she was peddling.'

'If you knew about the drugs, why didn't you report it to the police?'

She stared at me. 'And land up dead? You should grow up. What makes you think the police aren't involved? Money can keep anybody quiet, but fear works for me.'

'You seem to be the oracle, Alice. How did he get the drugs over here?'

'I dunno, but over the years he's had a constant supply of young Thai girls. I reckon they were bringing it in.'

A knock on the door and the appearance of Mark signalled an end to our conversation. I was to escort the discharged patients off the premises and then go for a coffee break.

I used my coffee break to go to my room to ring David. I guessed he'd be at work, but he'd have access to a computer and information that I couldn't get hold of.

'Are you busy?' I asked.

'Not too busy to speak to you, Kate.'

'Good. I need some info.'

'I guessed it wasn't my body you were after. What can I do for you?'

'I need information on methamphetamines.'

'Uppers?'

'Yes.'

'Why?'

'Because the staff at Fair Acres seem particularly fond of them.'

'Leave it alone, Kate. Drop it.'

'No. I've got this far – I'm not stopping now.'

'I can't talk now,' he said, 'but where drugs are concerned, many people have a weakness, and the police are only human – some are greedy, some are weak and some are bloody dangerous.'

'That's true enough,' I said, 'but I'm leaving on Sunday. If the police really want to make arrests, they should bust the party on Saturday night.'

'Where's it being held?'

Before I'd had a chance to tell him, the line went dead. My pay-as-you-go mobile phone had died through lack of funds. A little lifeline had been tweaked away.

Twenty-Seven

On Friday afternoon I was allowed off duty at two p.m. I was relieved to be able to escape. Fair Acres was in its death throes and the atmosphere changed from bravado and gung-ho cheerfulness to misery and depression and back again like a sheet in the wind.

Finishing early seemed an ideal opportunity to see young Brett again – and the new baby. There were one or two questions I'd failed to ask.

It was a dismal day with a grey sky and low clouds. There was little traffic and even less people. I arrived just after five and the sight of the house, with every room lit, cheered me. It was Pam who answered the door to me. 'It is nice to see you,' she said. She looked pale but happy.

'How's the baby?' I asked as she ushered me in.

'She's smashing. Been as good as gold. I'm beginning to get over the shock. The neighbours have been fantastic. I haven't had to buy a thing.'

In the living room, Brett and his dad sat watching a martial-arts DVD.

'Turn that bloody thing off,' said Pam loudly. 'We've got a visitor.'

Brett mumbled, 'Hi,' and stood up and shook my hand. 'Fancy a cuppa?' he asked.

While the tea was being made, Pam and I went upstairs to admire the baby. The room smelt of baby oil and baby. She lay in a pink-lined basket cot on a stand. In a few days, she'd obviously put on weight. Her cheeks were pink and chubby and we stood and watched her for a few minutes. I hoped she'd wake up so that I could hold her, but she slept on. 'Have you decided on a name?' I asked.

'Chelsy,' she said.

'After the football team?'

'No, after Prince Harry's girlfriend.'

'Lovely,' I murmured.

Downstairs, we drank tea and ate chocolate biscuits and then I had to ask to speak to Brett privately. 'About the accident, is it?' asked Pam.

I nodded. Brett flashed an anxious look at his mother.

She responded with, 'Go in the kitchen, you little toe-rag, and tell the bleeding truth.'

268

Brett perched on a kitchen stool at the breakfast bar, looking nervous and uncomfortable.

'You'll have to get used to being asked questions about that night,' I said quietly.

'I'm sick of it,' he said. 'Do you think I'll do time?'

'You've got a previous conviction, haven't you?' I asked.

'Yeah, but I only got a caution. Taking and driving away. I was only twelve.'

I sat uncomfortably on a stool next to him, and I could tell I was too close for his comfort. I wanted him to feel a little edgy and uneasy, so that his memory was sharper and he'd answer more quickly, in order to make his escape.

'Think back,' I said. 'It's a November night. Dark. Not much traffic. You're driving along...' I broke off. 'What are you doing?'

'I'm driving. That's a stupid frigging question.'

'Are you listening to the radio?'

'No.'

'So, you're driving along in silence.'

'I didn't say that.'

'What were you doing?'

'I was listening to a tape.'

'Was it loud?'

'Yeah. You'd think it was loud.'

'Why?'

'You're old.'

'Fine. So you're driving along, getting towards Finches Wood. Is there any other traffic?'

'No ... What do you mean by traffic?'

'Any vehicle at all.'

'Oh, yeah, well, there was a motorbike that overtook me.'

'What type?'

'Dunno. Big, pricey-looking.'

'Did you see the rider?'

Brett's opinion of that question showed in his face. 'He zoomed past me. He must have been doing eighty at least. He was just a black flash.'

'Black leathers? Black helmet?'

'Yeah. Now I think back.'

'So, you carried on listening to your tape and driving at a respectable speed?'

'Yeah.'

'Was it raining?'

'It was a bit.'

'Did you have your wipers on?'

'No. It wasn't that bad,' he said irritably. 'I'm getting fed up with this.'

'In court it'll be worse,' I said. 'Were you fed up that night? Down in the dumps? Agitated?'

'No. I like driving. I was OK.'

270

'Even though you'd had a row with your girlfriend?'

'Who told you that?'

'You did.'

'I don't frigging remember. You're trying to trick me.'

'I'm not, Brett. I'm just trying to get at the truth.'

His lower lip began to tremble. 'Look, I've told you everything. There was this car parked by the woods. The lights were off. The road is narrower there. Maybe I did drive too close to the car, but I didn't expect the frigging door to open just as I was passing. I was doing sixty – what could I do?'

'Don't get upset,' I said. 'Telling the truth will only help your case.'

'I shouldn't have reported it – that was my mistake.'

'That's in your favour,' I said. 'What time *exactly* did you report it?'

'Six o'clock in the morning. We didn't go to bed that night. I was in a terrible state. I couldn't stop shaking.'

'When you hit the car door and Trina Brampton and then drove on – what were you thinking?'

He stared at me as if I were speaking in Mandarin Chinese. Finally he said, 'I wasn't thinking straight, was I? I know it sounds stupid now, but me main worry was that my dad would kill me. He's always lecturing me on driving. My hands were shaking and my heart was banging in me ears and I felt weird. If I hadn't felt so bad, I would have driven on, but I had to stop to check it had really happened. I couldn't believe it.' His eyes had filled with tears and he brushed his face with his hands.

'You're doing well,' I said. 'You stopped, that's the important thing. How far on from the crash did you stop?'

'I don't know,' he snapped.

'Did you get as far as the nearest junction?'

'No. I s'pose it was a few hundred yards. Does it frigging matter?'

'It will do in court. They measure the distance.'

He folded his arms in a gesture of childish defiance.

'I am trying to help you remember,' I said. 'You stopped the car. What did you do then?'

Silence. For a few moments I thought he'd stopped cooperating, then he muttered, 'I sat there staring into space. I couldn't stop shaking. Then I got it together and got out of the car and looked back.'

'What did you see?'

'I saw this bloke leaning over the body.'

'Did he kneel down as if checking her

breathing?'

'Yeah,' he said thoughtfully. 'He was kneeling down.'

'Was it raining then?'

'Yeah. I remember it was running down my face.'

'How long did you stand there?'

'Not long. I saw the bloke, thought he might see me, and I really lost me bottle. I got back in the car and drove home.'

'Just one more question, Brett,' I said.

'What?'

'What makes you so sure the person you saw that night was male?'

There was a long pause. 'I dunno really. He looked sort of bulky.'

'Did he wear a hat?'

'It was a hood, I think ... I don't bloody know – I'm not sure.'

'Would you like to be sure? After all, if Trina Brampton was forced out of the car into your path, you can't be held to blame.'

'How can I be sure *now*?'

'Tonight, when it's dark, I could drive you to the exact spot. It could really jog your memory.'

He shrugged. 'OK. I s'pose so.' He obviously wasn't keen, but if it jogged his memory, the trip could be worthwhile.

After a protracted goodbye and explaining

our 'trip' to Pam, I drove back to Fair Acres and went straight to my room. I phoned David but he was in a meeting, I phoned Hubert but he was conducting a funeral. I watched TV for a while and went into a trance-like state watching yet another 'house' programme, featuring ever better holiday homes that few can afford. My bank account could furnish a strong cardboard box and little else, but I had no real desire to nest-build – I just wanted to stay at Humberstone. That didn't seem likely, and thoughts of Shirley-Marie and the wedding march still turned my stomach.

My disappointment that neither David nor Hubert were available was short-lived, because there was a timid tap at my door. It was Suki, looking worried.

'Have you seen Lorna? I can't find her. She's upset...' She broke off as if changing her mind about telling me why she was upset.

'What about the staff cafeteria, have you looked there?'

She shook her head.

'I'll come with you,' I said. 'If Lorna's anywhere, she'll be near food.'

Even serious Suki smiled.

We found Lorna sitting with Alice and looking cheerful. 'Everything's half price,' she said. A plateful of cream cakes sat between the two of them. Normally I love cream cakes, but the sight of the cream around Lorna's mouth quenched my desire. We sat down with them and Suki went off to fetch tea.

'Is everyone coming to the party?' I asked

'Wouldn't miss it,' said Alice. 'I like seeing people make fools of themselves. Mind you, I don't know why they've changed the venue.'

'Changed?' I queried. 'Where to?'

'Here – in the cafeteria. I reckon our dear Louise wanted it here. She's like that. Has to be in charge.'

'What do you think, Lorna?' I asked.

Lorna wiped her mouth with the back of her hand. 'I'm not bothered,' she said. 'I expect the food will be as good.'

Suki returned with teas and a sandwich, and sat quietly watching us. Looking directly at Alice, I said, 'I heard a rumour the other day that Trina Brampton and Rupert were having an affair. What do you think?'

She laughed. 'That's an old one. He was the sort to bed any woman under forty. Some men are like that.'

'Brian Brampton seemed the possessive type,' I said. 'I'm surprised he didn't know what was going on.'

Alice laughed dryly. 'Of course he knew. I reckon he put her up to it.'

'You're just guessing, Alice,' said Lorna. 'You don't know what was going on then any more than we did.'

'Maybe you're wrong there. I saw them together.'

'When?' demanded Lorna. 'When did you see them together?'

'I saw them in the summer in Finches Wood, near to where she died.'

Lorna's mouth dropped open. 'You've never told us this before. And anyway, how could you see them? You haven't got a car, and a social worker brings you into work.'

'She's not *just* a social worker, she's a friend, a real friend.' Alice's eyes were bright and her hand shook as she picked up her cup.

'So, you were with your social-worker *friend*,' persisted Lorna. 'What were you doing in the woods?'

'We'd just come for an afternoon spin on her motorbike. We had a picnic and we were just planning to leave when we saw Brian, Trina and Rupert some distance away, but both men had an arm around Trina like she was ... shared.'

'You've got a filthy mind,' snapped Lorna.

Alice's returning smile was more of a

sneer. 'At least I have my mind back now. I'm recovering. You've lost yours. Your stomach does your thinking. I bet it's the only stomach in the world that hears voices.'

'You bitch!' said Lorna between gritted teeth. She stood up abruptly and as she did so her heavy plastic chair tipped backwards with a clatter. She lumbered away, head down, not looking, but knocking into people and chairs. She was closely followed by Suki.

Alice looked me straight in the eye. 'I'm not sorry. Lorna had a right crush on that Rupert. Especially after he offered to operate on her. An operation wouldn't give her any more self-control, would it? Rupert was an arsehole and Victoria was a fool for putting up with him. She made him worse. Louise would have sorted him out.'

'Why Louise?'

Alice looked surprised that I needed to ask. 'It was a toss up over which one he'd marry, and Victoria won.'

'You're the oracle, Alice. Why did he choose Victoria?'

'Money, of course. She worked in finance, didn't she? Bound to have quite a bit stashed away.'

'So, was there bad feeling between them?'

'If there was, it never showed. They kept each other at arm's length.'

Although I knew Alice put her own rather warped interpretation on everything, she was worth listening to. The fact that her social worker had a motorbike was of little interest and unlikely to be the same bike that overtook Brett the night Trina died. Unlikely, but not impossible. Did the police even know that a motorbike had passed by a short time before the accident? The bike rider could be a potential witness. But my time at Fair Acres was running out and I was as near to solving three murders as I was to explaining the meaning of life.

Twenty-Eight

By ten p.m. I was driving a silent, maybe sullen, Brett to Finches Wood. I would have preferred it to rain, so that conditions were replicated, but the night was dry, although the clouds were low.

There was little traffic and I was able to keep to a slow speed. As we approached the road leading to the woods, I asked Brett to tell me where exactly he saw Trina's car.

'It looks different from the passenger seat,' he said miserably. There was no traffic around, so I slowed to about ten miles per hour. Then my eye caught something lying against a tree close to the roadside. The dead flowers with the obliterated message were still there.

'I think it was here,' I said.

'Could be,' he said dully.

We left the car then, and began walking. Brett's head was down, his shoulders hunched. The night seemed to be getting colder but occasionally I saw that patches of daffodils were showing a little yellow in the gloom.

'Think about where you stopped,' I said. 'Was there a landmark – anything?'

'Landmark? That's a joke. There are only trees and bushes.'

'And pathways,' I added.

We walked on for another couple of hundred yards and then abruptly Brett stopped.

'There,' he said, pointing towards a pathway. 'That pine tree, I remember that.'

I'd already decided that I was going to walk back to the car, leaving Brett standing with his back to me. 'Give me a couple of minutes to get back to the car and then turn around and try to remember what you actually saw that night.'

'Waste of time,' he muttered, and I had to agree – now that we were here, it did seem just that.

I hurried back to the car and pulled the hood of my jacket over my head, before bending down as if over Trina's body. I saw Brett turn and look back at me for several seconds. Then he turned his head to one side, leaned over and vomited.

Once back in the car, although his complexion was ashen, he said he felt better, and I gave him my emergency bottle of mineral water.

'Did you remember anything?' I asked after he'd slugged at the water.

'Yeah,' he said thoughtfully. 'I couldn't tell from that distance if you were a man or a woman. But whoever it was wasn't wearing a hood – it was a helmet.'

'You're sure?'

'I'm sure. There was a slight shine to it.'

'That's a real help,' I said. 'Thanks.'

As I dropped him off at his house, I still had one more question to ask.

'When you stopped the car and got out, did you switch the tape off?'

He looked taken aback. 'I should have done,' he said in a nervous rush. 'But I didn't know what I was doing. I just got back in the car and drove off, like if I got home it hadn't happened.'

'It's not a crime,' I said. 'But you might have heard the sound of a motorbike leaving the scene if you had.'

The following morning was the day of the party. I met Lorna in the kitchen and she seemed more cheerful. 'Tonight's party,' she said, 'is like the sinking of the *Titanic* with the band playing on.'

'Are we having a disco?' I asked.

'We do usually,' she said. 'Sometimes there's a karaoke as well.'

'Should be quite a jolly do in the circumstances,' I said.

'The drink will be flowing, that's for sure,' she said.

I made my toast and tea with Lorna watching me, then I broached the subject of the motorbike. 'Do you know anyone who has a motorbike?' I asked.

'Fancy a fast ride, do you?' she asked, with just a hint of suspicion in her voice.

'No. I've often thought I'd like to have a go on one before deciding to buy. I just thought you might know someone who might advise me.'

She shook her head. 'We could find out tonight.'

Back in my room, I ate my breakfast and began to pack my things. My brief undercover activity was nearly over, with a startling lack of success. Apart from the horrific discovery of my client's body and the realization that there was a drug problem at Fair Acres, I was no further on in discovering who killed or had a hand in the death of Trina and Rupert. Or for that matter Victoria.

A phone call from David interrupted my thoughts. His first words were a shock.

'I'll be escorting you to the party,' he said.

'But you haven't been invited,' I responded

churlishly.

'I'm more in the know than you are, and I want to be there to—'

'To what?' I interrupted him. 'Look after me? I don't need looking after.'

'You can be bloody hard work, Kate. I was going to say – if you'd let me finish – that I wanted to take you somewhere swish for a couple of days. I've got time off and Hubert's intended has landed.'

I swore under my breath. I felt as if my home and livelihood had been taken away in one fell swoop on the UK.

'Are you still there?' asked David.

'I'm still here. How swish do you mean?'

'At least a four-star hotel.'

'Sounds like an offer I can't refuse.'

'Don't be too grateful, will you?' said David.

I agreed to meet him in the reception hall at eight, and I heard him mutter, 'Love you,' as he put down the phone.

Later that day, I drove into town, looking for an outfit to wear to the party. It was a protracted affair, and how anyone can enjoy shopping for clothes is beyond me. First you search the racks, then find the only size not available is yours. Finally, having made a selection, you have to try the item on.

Stripping off in front of a full up-close mirror must be the most depressing shopping experience. Revealed in harsh strip lighting is a pasty white skin, a greying bra, knicker elastic beginning to unravel, and little bulges everywhere. You hope the dress, top or trousers will somehow transform you. It never does. The shoes are wrong, your hair is mussed, a waistband is too tight, but if you have a larger size it'll be baggy. Tops are either too long or too short, too tight or too loose. I'd reached this point of hysteria by the third shop. When I finally found a silky pair of black trousers and silvery top that didn't look too tight and tarty, or loose and mumsy, a wave of relief spread over me – I'd done it.

My euphoria lasted only a few minutes, as I remembered the arrival of Shirley-Marie. I felt virtually homeless, like a refugee. Hubert, always so keen to help and support me, was now preoccupied and far too busy to return my calls. Perhaps I'd become an irritation, an obstacle to his happiness. The only answer, I decided, was to plan a holiday, somewhere warm where I could make a few decisions about my future. In the meantime, I hoped to make some progress with what I now saw was a hopeless investigation. I'd been too confident and ambitious. Errant husbands and missing persons would in future be the peak of my ambition.

Once back in my room, I checked I'd packed everything and lay down for a nap. The occasional party I do attend, I'm wilting by ten thirty and can never quite pace my drinks. For me it's a few drinks downed quickly and then I stop. After midnight I'm tired but sober. Tonight I wanted to join in but keep alert, because I was sure there was still something I could discover.

At eight p.m. I stood in reception, watching as staff and guests began arriving. Most were strangers, although I saw Polly and Alice in the throng and waved at them. Polly wore a white, strapless, backless, hardly there at all dress and looked golden and wonderful. Even Alice looked striking in a gold top and black skirt. Feeling like a cup short of a saucer in reception, I decided to wait for a while in the car park, hoping to see David arrive. At eight thirty-five, and thoroughly chilled by fifteen minutes in the cold night air, I decided to wait no longer but join the party.

The staff cafeteria was almost unrecognizable. The strip lighting had been exchanged for soft lamplight. The tables were now arranged around the room, and in one corner the disco was being set up complete with disco lights. A large banner suspended from the ceiling proclaimed – *Not the End*.

The women looked glamorous and hardly recognizable out of uniform. Louise Booth in particular, in a red off-the-shoulder little number, looked stunning. She stood alone, glass in hand, talking to the disc jockey. I hoped she was telling him to keep the volume low, as I wanted to hear as much gossip as possible. I hoped that, being dressed up, when Brian Brampton did see me he wouldn't recognize me as the person he had followed.

I was making my way to a table stacked with alcohol when Beryl and Julie, like conjoined twins, almost knocked me over. They must have had more than one *aperitif* before the party started. They were loud and hysterically giggling. At the table, Beryl ladled me out a large glass of punch. I sipped it warily. It was delicious.

The disco started up then, not quite on full volume, and moments later began the flashing disco lights. The party atmosphere had begun, although, as the lights settled on faces and threw them into shadows and strange colours, I found it vaguely sinister.

There was no sign of Suki or Lorna.

Twenty-Nine

After the second full glass of punch, I began to care less about David's non-appearance. He was often late, and I wasn't the only one waiting for her man to arrive. Polly stood near the door and I noticed her glancing at her expensive looking wristwatch. The disco lights played on her face, but even that couldn't mask her anxious expression.

I made my way over to her, between groups of people I didn't recognize. 'Are you waiting for Brian?' I asked in her ear, to overcome the loud throb of the music.

'Oh, hi, Kate. Yeah. He said he might be a bit late.'

'I'm waiting for someone,' I said, 'and he's already an hour and a half late.'

We stood people-watching for a while, not able to chat because of the volume of the disco music. 'I think I'll phone him,' she said loudly. As she walked away, I waited a second or two and then followed her just in time to see her go through the swing doors of the kitchen. I peeped in. More food, covered in cling film, was laid out in the preparation area. The chrome and stainless steel sparkled, and although the bass sounds still reverberated, at least it was dulled. I tiptoed towards the slightly ajar chef's office door, and a wisp of smoke from Polly's cigarette wafted into the main kitchen. Polly sounded as if she were leaving a message. By the door, I could hear her say, 'Anyway, ring me. I'm missing you.'

I scuttled away and resumed people-watching by the door. I wasn't planning on phoning David. If he couldn't be bothered to turn up on time, it was his loss.

By now it was ten p.m. and Alice's voice carried even above the disco. 'Like your *friend*,' she yelled as Mark Alba appeared with a pale young man in tow. Mark looked embarrassed but went straight to the drinks table and began pouring himself and his companion large glasses of red wine. I walked over and picked up the punch ladle.

'Watch that stuff, my darling,' said Mark, patting my arm. 'It's truly lethal.' Then he turned to his companion. 'Kate, this is Paul. Paul – Kate.'

Paul kissed my hand. 'I've heard these parties turn into orgies. When does it start?'

'This is my first time,' I said. 'I'm living in

288

hope, but an orgy seems a long way off.'

'You wait and see,' said Mark in my ear. 'Keep an eye on our cool and collected director of nursing.'

I looked over to where she was sitting at a table with two grey men in grey suits.

Mark followed my line of vision. 'Those two are surgeons,' he said, 'both due for retirement and, believe me, well past their sell-by date.'

I ladled myself another half glass of punch and sipped at it slowly. The pony-tailed disc jockey was announcing, in a pause between records, that there would be an interval in fifteen minutes, when the buffet would commence. Anything he said after that I missed, because, although he shouted, the microphone distorted his voice.

'Have you heard, dotty Doris has been released,' said Mark. 'No charge.'

'What about Dale Dutchman?'

'I heard he was released after twenty-four hours.'

'I'm glad. He was set up.'

'Let's not dwell on that,' said Mark. 'Our sinking ship has sunk. Not a patient body left in the building – so let's make the most of it. I've got some E if you want it.'

'No thanks,' I said, as if being offered some ecstasy was as regular as having the occasional ciggie. 'The punch will see me through.'

Paul spoke then in a high-pitched, affected way. 'I've got some wacky baccy if you'd prefer that.'

'Makes me cough,' I said, 'but thanks anyway.'

During the interval, the disco lights were switched off and Polly appeared by my side looking worried. 'Come outside, Kate. I want to talk to you.' Outside, in the brighter light of the corridor, I could see she'd been crying. 'What on earth's the matter?' I asked.

'He's gone,' she said tearfully.

'Brian?'

'Yes. I drove to his place. I don't live with him, but he gave me a key. He's packed his cases and gone.'

'Did he leave a note?'

'No. Nothing. I thought he was in love with me. I can't believe it. I've been such a fool.'

'We've all been there,' I said.

'Not as often as I have.'

I put an arm around her. 'Come on, let's have another drink.'

'I need more than a drink,' she said bleakly.

As we sat at an empty table with our drinks, I couldn't help wondering if David had also done a runner. I tried his mobile, but it was switched off, and I didn't bother leaving a message. 'You too,' observed Polly.

I was disappointed that David hadn't answered for two reasons – one, of course, was personal, the other because I wanted his professional advice. Should I ring the local police and report that Brian Brampton was probably on his way to East Midlands airport? Or was it too late anyway?

'You don't have to sit with me,' said Polly. 'There's a guy on that corner table who's been eyeballing you for ages.'

'Really? Are you sure he's not looking at you?'

'He's definitely looking your way, Kate.'

'Who is he?'

'I think he's a pharmacist.'

'Oh,' I said. 'Well, I'll go a bit closer then. Are you sure you'll be all right?'

'Yeah. I'll join Lorna and Suki – they look as miserable as I feel.'

Lorna and Suki had made an appearance, and sat eating silently on their own. By their expressions, they could well have been at a funeral rather than a party.

The guy at the corner table returned my smile, so I had nothing to lose by joining him, and he might give me some valuable information. I guessed he was about thirty-five – and not bad-looking, in a slim, scholarly way. He was wearing a suit and tie, which was a rarity, because whilst most of the women looked glamorous, the men seemed to have dressed down.

'Hi,' I said with a cheerful smile. 'Do you mind if I sit here for a while? It would be nice to talk to someone I don't work with.'

'Fine by me. Can I get you a drink?'

'Yes please. I've been sticking to the punch.'

'I think,' he said, 'that's a magic tureen. I've watched people walk away with their large glasses of punch, yet I haven't seen anyone refill it.'

I giggled and I knew I'd had too much to drink. Soon I'd be talking loudly and too much, then I'd probably get maudlin. I took a deep breath and tried to compose myself.

His name was Ian Benson and, although he was a qualified pharmacist, he worked as a drug representative managing the Midlands. 'I like travelling,' he explained. I told him a little about me, as I struggled to find a subtle way to ask him how much he knew about methamphetamines. When in doubt, an imaginary friend comes in useful. Jackie, I told him, had been abroad and had come back with a huge supply of 'uppers', which she now seemed addicted to.

'Did she go to Thailand?' asked Ian.

I nodded.

'I don't know the situation there now,' he said, 'but two years back Thailand was flooded with methamphetamines made in labs in Burma. Cheaper to produce, easier to smuggle and market than heroin, and it soon caught on. It's cheap, can be eaten or ground up and smoked.'

The disco music started up more loudly than ever, and Ian moved nearer to me.

'How does this stuff get here?' I asked.

'Human mules smuggle it in, or it's put in tyre wheels – who knows? Smugglers are very ingenious.'

We sipped at our drinks, watching as people took to the floor. Louise Booth had begun to dance suggestively ... and whilst she was capable of dancing, she was definitely high.

'The Thais call it ya ba,' he said loudly in my ear. 'Which means "crazy medicine".'

'Crazy sums Jackie up. Is there—'

The sound of a mobile phone interrupted me. It was Ian's. 'It's my wife,' he said. 'Do excuse me.'

Story of my life, I thought, especially when, fifteen minutes later, he still hadn't returned.

I wandered around for a while, found two couples getting close in the kitchen, and was walking back when my mobile rang. It was Hubert.

'You two having a good time?' he asked cheerfully.

'David hasn't arrived,' I said.

There was a protracted silence. 'He rang me from outside Brian Brampton's place – about eight p.m. That's where the party is ... isn't it?'

'No,' I said weakly. 'The venue was changed. It's at Fair Acres. I told him to meet me in reception. Why the hell didn't he ring me?'

'He said he tried, but there was no reply, so he rang me instead.'

'Something's happened to him ... I know it has.'

'Calm down, Kate. He's probably fine. He's a cop – he can take care of himself.'

'I've got to find him. I'll speak later.'

I knew I had to look for him, but I'd had too much to drink, so I desperately needed a driver. There in a corner, with the disco lights flickering in their faces, sat Lorna and Suki, both drinking Coca Cola. I rushed over to their table. 'You drive, don't you, Lorna?'

'Yes. I drive.'

'You haven't had a drink?'

'No.'

'Will you drive me to Brian Brampton's house?'

'He's not there. Polly told us.'

'My boyfriend David was there at eight o'clock. It's eleven now and that makes him missing. Please ... I'm sure something's happened to him.'

Reluctantly Lorna said, 'OK. Come on, Suki.'

Suki stood up. 'I don't mind,' she said. 'We can come back later.'

Lorna squashed herself in the front seat of my car, and I sat beside her to direct her.

'I know where he lives,' she said. 'Polly told me.'

My stomach was churning and, as hard as I tried, I could not put a positive spin on David's disappearance. Neither Lorna nor Suki were chatty, and Lorna drove as slowly as an elderly vicar, so the journey seemed interminable.

The house was dark and deserted. There was no sign of David's car, and yet I felt I ought to check out the gardens and peep through the letter box in case David lay injured inside.

It was as I was getting back into the car that I saw a piece of paper in the gutter. I picked it up and recognized it as a wrapper from David's favourite chewing gum. Somehow it seemed like a bad omen. 'This place is jinxed,' Doris had said to me. She'd been right, and now it had become personal.

Thirty

'Where to now?' asked Lorna.

I had no idea. My mind was blank. I tried imagining David arriving, thinking he was one of the first guests, knocking at the door and seeing the suitcases, and perhaps deciding to follow him.

'Do you know the way to East Midlands airport?' I asked.

'It's about twenty miles,' said a disgruntled Lorna.

'I'm sorry ... please.'

She gave a huge sigh, but drove off at a slightly increased speed. I turned round to see that Suki had her eyes closed. She could have been pretending to be asleep but she seemed genuinely out of it. Lorna drove in silence, but she continually rummaged in her pocket and then tried surreptitiously to eat her goodies. 'What *are* you eating?' I asked.

'Peanuts and raisins,' she said.

I looked at her sharply, but she didn't notice – her eyes were firmly fixed on the road ahead. Peanuts and raisins ... peanuts!

The word kept reverberating in my head, but I forced myself to concentrate on the road. Perhaps David's car had broken down. Around each corner I half expected to see him flagging down a passing motorist.

'Why do you think your boyfriend has gone to the airport?' asked Lorna, with her mouth half full.

'He's gone after Brian Brampton.'

'Why would he do that?'

'He's a cop.'

'You didn't tell us that before. I thought he was an undertaker.'

'Policemen aren't always popular, and if I tell people, they think he's going to check their car tax or book them for smoking hash or whatever – so I keep quiet.'

'I get your point,' she said.

She drove on for a while, and at the junction that signalled it was ten miles to East Midlands airport, she turned left instead of right.

'Where are you going?' I demanded, my voice far from level.

'Brampton isn't there,' she said. 'I'll take you near to where he is.'

I stared for a while, my mind racing. I was scared now, really scared. Lorna's face was set in a grimly determined expression. I turned around to see if Suki was still asleep.

She wasn't, she was smiling at me. A knowing little smirk. I turned back, realizing they were in this together.

'You killed Rupert, didn't you?' I said, trying to keep the tremor from my voice.

Lorna stopped the car in a lay-by and grabbed my wrist, but she didn't look at me, she stared straight ahead. 'I don't know who you really are,' she said, 'but you've got in our way. And yes, I did stuff a prune with a peanut and I offered it to him like a poisoned apple. He took the bait and died.'

'But why?'

She continued to stare straight ahead, and when she did speak, her voice was emotionless.

'For so many reasons, Kate. If not then, it would have been some other time. When I was nineteen and slim, we had a brief affair. I got pregnant and he didn't want to know. I had the baby aborted. Then, years later, we met up again. He couldn't acknowledge he'd even met me before, but he did promise me that he'd operate on me to make my stomach smaller, so that I wouldn't be able to eat so much.'

'But surely *that* was a good reason for keeping him alive.'

'It was,' she said, 'until I overheard him talking to Rav in the chef's office that night at the party. Rav wasn't too happy about being the anaesthetist – he thought I would be at risk.'

'Perhaps he was right.'

'Maybe he was,' said Lorna slowly. 'But that bastard Decker-White said, "If the fat cow dies … she dies".'

'I'm sorry,' I said.

'Yes, so was he. My face was the last one he saw.'

She started up the car and released the grip on my arm. 'Take me back to Fair Acres – please, Lorna.'

'No can do,' she said. 'You haven't done us any harm, but now you know, you're a threat.'

I'd half decided that when she next slowed down I'd try to make a run for it, and suddenly visions of Trina Brampton doing exactly the same thing sprang to mind. If she'd killed Rupert and Trina … what about Victoria? I was beginning to panic, my stomach churned, my mouth dried, and the acrid taste of punch rose in my throat.

She drove on for a couple of miles – a straight road, grass verges, trees everywhere – then she turned down a pathway into woods, on and on, and then she stopped. She grabbed my wrist again and I heard Suki getting out of the car.

'We have one more thing to attend to before we catch our plane tomorrow,' said Lorna. 'One more bitch. Victoria was a mistake that Suki made. She thought she was in the know about the drugs racket, but she wasn't. Victoria was just blind and stupid, whereas Louise Booth is greedy.'

I stayed silent, for now I had seen where the car was parked – by a river.

'I might be grossly fat,' she continued, 'and greedy for food, but my greed doesn't harm anyone. People like Decker-White and Booth and Brampton – their greed harms thousands. They deserve to die.'

I was about to plead my case when Lorna signalled to Suki to open the car door. As she opened it, Lorna pushed and Suki pulled. Although I tried to resist, Suki was stronger than I thought and she nearly dislocated my shoulder. Soon I was on the ground and Lorna and Suki were kicking me into the river. The shock of the cold water took my breath away as if a boulder had hit my chest. For several seconds, I thought death was imminent. I couldn't see and I could hardly breathe, but I heard the car being driven away.

I was in total darkness, struggling to breathe, although my head was above water, and suddenly my toe touched something solid. The river was more of a stream. I scrabbled to my feet. I'd lost one shoe but I was at least upright. I managed to get to the bank, and lay like a dying dolphin, trying to breathe normally. I felt desperately cold and knew that if I didn't get help or find shelter, I wouldn't make it back to the main road. Hypothermia would set in very quickly, especially in wet clothes. I had to keep going. Every minute counted. I tried shouting for help, but knew it was pointless. I could see nothing but the dark shapes of trees and bushes. The ground was hard and crunchy and sparkly with frost. I was on some sort of path, but was I even going in the right direction?

After only a few minutes, I'd begun to flag. My fingers and toes burnt with cold and I'd stopped shivering and that was a bad sign. Soon I knew I'd start to get confused or lie down and go to sleep. Keep walking, keep walking was my mantra, but then I began to see things. I thought I saw the slight gleam of a car between the trees. I tried to walk faster but my legs were leaden and, although I tried to make out the number plate, my eyes wouldn't focus properly. It wasn't until I actually touched the car that I believed it was real. But by then I had seen who was in the passenger seat. It was David.

Thirty-One

I didn't scream or cry out, even though I could see he was dead. I was either trembling or shivering, I didn't know which, and I hardly had the strength to open the car door. Once in the driver's seat, I had a strong urge to put my head on David's shoulder and sleep, even die. I didn't care any more. He was dead because of my carelessness. The keys weren't in the ignition and, although I was out of the wind and the cold air, my clothes hung on me like bands of ice, chilling body and mind.

Still numb with cold, I pressed my hand over David's. Our hands were both white and seemed equally cold, but I wasn't dead yet. I imagined him saying, 'Get a grip, Kate. Stay awake.' Sleep still seemed to me to be the most comfortable option, and I turned my head to look at the back seat. On it were two copies of the *Daily Telegraph* and a car blanket. 'Thanks, David,' I said, kissing his cheek as if he were still alive. I noticed now the blood that had seeped from his chest to his groin. Anger settled over me, giving me a vague sense of warmth. They would *not* get away. I leant over and began stripping off my wet clothes. The front seat was soaked, so I scrabbled naked and clumsy over to the back seat, where I wound the pages of the *Daily Telegraph* around me. I slid my feet under the car mats and hoped I was safe from wet rot and frostbite.

After my exertions, I felt only slightly warmer, but my mind was clearer. What now? How many hours could I last? If I slept, would I die? Was I warm enough now, and strong enough, to search the boot of the car? This is as good as it gets, I thought, and opened the car door to a blast of freezing air.

Opening the boot was a struggle, but worth it. David's padded jacket and overnight bag were in there. I was saved, but mixed with the euphoria was still the guilt that I was alive and David wasn't.

I put the jacket on, grabbed the bag and got back in the back seat. Excitedly I unzipped the bag. Inside were two sets of underpants, two T-shirts, two pairs of trousers, one formal shirt, two pairs of socks, and a box of tissues, a toilet bag, a bar of chocolate, a packet of sandwiches and a can of Coke. Even in the midst of tragedy, it felt as if I'd won the lottery. I slipped on both pairs of socks and both pairs of T-shirts and underpants. It reminded me of being a small child at the seaside, coming in from the sea and feeling cold and covered in sand, and my mother would diligently rid me of the sand and then slip on vest and pants. That cosy warmth was how I felt now. Adding a pair of his black denims felt like bliss.

In the zipped compartments of his bag, I found a notebook, unused, two biros, a travel clock and a mobile phone and charger. Please God, let it work. My hand trembled as I dialled nine-nine-nine.

As I was helped into an ambulance, I could see in the distance the glint of a black Jaguar, and police surrounding it. I guessed Brampton's body was in there. It was only by chance that I'd come across David's car and not the Jag. I had a feeling David, even in death, had helped me.

I sat in A&E for two hours, wrapped in blankets and waiting for a check-up from a doctor. My vital signs, it seemed, were somewhat depressed, and my body temperature was still subnormal. A detective constable called Vincent Turner, known as Vin, took my preliminary statement. I felt sure that Lorna and Suki driving my car would be found quickly – after all, Lorna was easily recognizable.

As a source of information, Vin was as useful as if he'd been in a call centre in Bombay for the last year. The only info he could give me was that a raid on Fair Acres had been planned.

I began wandering around with my blankets trailing and David's trousers dragging the floor, like someone demented. Vin followed me around, close as a young puppy. A&E wasn't that busy, and physically I felt fine. Mentally, though, I was disturbed. I didn't want justice, I wanted revenge. The pair from hell had taken David from me and killed at least three others, and I wanted to know why. But more than that I wanted them locked up – for ever.

Eventually a young doctor advanced on me with a stethoscope. A nurse retook my vital signs and I was told everything was normal and I was fit to leave. Of course, everything wasn't normal. My mind wasn't normal. I wanted to cry for David, who I imagined on some cold marble slab being picked over by a pathologist who hadn't known him and didn't care. But the tears wouldn't surface; they stayed somewhere in my chest, making me feel as if I wanted to explode.

Vin drove me back to Fair Acres. He was

very good at having a conversation about various sports with absolutely no input from me. I grunted occasionally and muttered, 'Really?' every so often, but I had no idea what he was talking about. I just let him drone on.

The car park was full of police cars, the hospital itself was a blaze of lights and a helicopter whirled overhead like a crazed bee. Vin led me into reception, which looked more like an airport lounge with well-delayed flights. Guests were either slumped in chairs or propped against walls, or curled up into balls and sleeping. I didn't look for familiar faces – what I wanted were my belongings and a quick exit.

Vin took me through to one of the administration offices and sat me down as if I were a very old lady. I didn't mind. I felt old, tired and slightly confused.

'You stay there,' said Vin, 'and I'll find a senior officer to talk to you.' He left and I sat staring into space. No thoughts crossed my mind, it was a blank page, and as hard as I tried, no words appeared on that page.

After a short time, a tall man in a crumpled grey suit, with stubble on his face and tired eyes, appeared. 'I'm Superintendent Gordon Roper. My condolences. I didn't know David, but I had spoken to him on the phone. We had kept him informed of our plans on the strict understanding that he told no one. This has been a very complex case involving the drug squad, the fraud squad and customs and excise. We had to wait for the right time...'

'Left it all too late, didn't you?'

'In hindsight, yes. But we wanted to catch everyone – users and, more importantly, the ringleaders.'

'Have you caught those evil bitches?'

'Yes. We caught them at East Midlands airport. They'd bought tickets to Thailand. But they won't be going anywhere now.'

'Why? Why did they do it?'

'We don't know. They're being interviewed now.'

'What about Louise? They were after her.'

'She's safe. It seemed they came looking for her, but she and a man friend had locked themselves in her office for some nookie, and the pair couldn't find her.'

'Has she been arrested?'

'Yes – for involvement in drug smuggling.'

'They were all at it, weren't they?'

'A large number were. If not dealing then using. It was a very lucrative business. Men like Decker-White and Brampton saw their little drug empire as their personal pension fund. Gradually they caught others in their greedy web.'

'What about police blindness and deafness?'

Superintendent Roper gave a little shrug, almost of defeat. 'I have to admit, that did occur. The police *are* part of the society we live in. Some get into debt, some into wife-beating, some into drugs. Many look for an easy way out. They begin their careers full of high ideals and good intentions. But some get tarnished along the way, even the top brass.'

Once more, creeping lassitude began to enfold me. I wanted to be in my own darkened room with a hot-water bottle and a duvet.

'There is someone to take you home,' he said. 'I'll wheel him in.'

When he'd gone, I closed my eyes and began to nod off. When I looked up suddenly, there stood Hubert. Immediately my eyes filled with tears, and as he put his arms round me, he said, 'Poor old Kate. Come on, let's get you home.' I cried even more then.

Hubert had come prepared, for he bedded me down in the back of his car with a pillow and blankets and the best treat of all, Jasper. With his little body shaking with excitement, tail wagging and licking my face, his only demand was lots of fuss. Within minutes, Jasper and I were cuddled up together fast asleep. It was only when I was woken up by a little yap from Jasper that I realized we were driving into Humberstone's car park. It was only then I remembered *her*.

'I'm not up to meeting Shirley-Marie,' I said as I raised myself into the upright position.

'You won't have to,' he said. 'She's gone. She only stayed one night.'

My jaw dropped in surprise. 'I'm so sorry.'

'No you're not, Kate. You're not sorry at all.'

'I'm sorry for your sake. What happened?'

'She said I'd not given her vital information about my circumstances.'

'Such as?'

'Jasper. I didn't mention him. Not only does she hate dogs. She's allergic to them. Within an hour of her being in the same room as Jasper, her face and eyes were swollen. She issued an ultimatum. Her or Jasper. So there was no contest. I looked at Jasper's little face and then at hers. Jasper was by far the better looking – and he doesn't need botox every few months.'

In spite of his loss and mine, we managed to laugh.

Days passed and the arrival of letters of condolence – and with them the realization that David wasn't going to walk through the door ever again – hit home. I knew I'd get over it in time, but time seemed to slow down, as if held back by guilt and sadness. Hubert too, of course, was equally melancholic. In his job, though, having a miserable expression was a positive advantage. We did talk often about David and the funeral. There being a murder case, his body was unlikely to be released for several weeks, but Hubert had been in touch with David's eldest sister, who lived on the south coast, and she was happy for the funeral to take place in Longborough. Hubert would be officiating and it would be a humanist service.

The arrival of a police car on Saturday morning seemed like a welcome diversion for both of us. The two uniformed officers, Inspector Malcolm Jacks and Sergeant Richard Howard from Longborough, sat in the kitchen with us drinking tea and saying nice things about David. I began to find it a strain, and eventually I said, 'What about his murderers?'

Inspector Jacks rested one hand on his rather large belly. 'We've only got the info second-hand,' he said. 'East Midlands police will get in touch with you when they have time, but the two women have been charged

with the murders of Decker-White and...'
He broke off. 'Have you got the notebook,
Sergeant?'

DS Howard fished in his jacket pocket,
produced a notebook and handed it over.
Jacks flicked it open with a flourish. 'I want
to get it right,' he said. 'The manslaughter of
Trina Brampton was the first, then the
murder of Rupert Decker-White and his
wife Victoria, and latterly the murder of
Brian Brampton and Inspector Todman.'

'I want to know *why*?' I said, getting irritat-
ed.

He peered at his notebook. 'It seems Suki
Kanda was the leader. Three years back, her
husband Don met Decker-White in a bar.
They got chatting. Don was working all
hours at the time, and Decker-White offered
him some *ya ba* to keep him going.' He
paused to glance at Hubert. 'I'd love another
cup of tea, mate.' Hubert looked none too
pleased, but he did put the kettle on.

'So, what happened?'

'Richard knows more about the drug scene
than me, he was in Thailand three years ago.
And because of that he was allowed to sit in
on the interviews. That's why he's here.'

DC Richard Howard ran a hand through
his spiky black hair. 'I'm not an expert,' he
said, 'but I've been to Thailand a few times.

I stay away from the tourist areas and live with a family that my sister got to know. So I learnt about the drug scene.'

Hubert poured tea, handed it round and then sat down to listen. 'I knew a teenager there,' Richard continued. 'He started on *ya ba* – just a couple of pills a day at first. Soon he was on twelve a day. I tried to help him – it seems the addictive nature of the drug is even stronger than heroin. These addicted kids soon have to turn to crime to fund the habit.'

'So, is it just the young who take the stuff?' I asked.

Richard shook his head. 'In 2001, the government estimated that eight hundred million pills were produced annually in Burma. That means thirteen pills for every Thai citizen. Rich, poor, young and old were getting addicted. So the government started a war on drugs – and that's where Suki Kanda's husband became involved.'

'What happened?'

Richard frowned. 'It was a bloodbath really. In their desperation to stop the drug dealers, there was what can only be described as a shoot-to-kill policy. In three months two thousand two hundred people were killed by police or hired guns. Innocent people were killed in the crossfire. These deaths were attributed to traffickers, but everyone knew that wasn't so. Unfortunately, Suki's husband was one of those shot. He's paralysed from the waist down. Before he became addicted to *ya ba*, he was relatively well off. Suki was more than bitter, and she held Decker-White responsible. Since he was a dealer, she could have easily got him arrested or killed, but she saw that, if she was to provide for her family, she needed to earn money. She decided to come to the UK and send money home. Decker-White, feeling some degree of remorse, also gave her a lump sum to tide the family over for a few weeks. She admits she was planning to kill him herself.'

'So Lorna killing him did her a favour,' I said. 'Why not stop there?'

'It seems, as the friendship between the pair grew, they decided between themselves to have their own war on drugs. The night Trina Brampton died, they suspected a big "drop" was happening in the woods. In fact, it seems Trina had been planning to meet an anaesthetist ... Rav?'

I nodded.

'He was late and arrived near their meeting point to find her dead in the road.'

'Was he on a motorbike?'

Richard looked surprised that I knew.

'Yeah. He keeps it in his garage. Doesn't use it often, but he did that night.'

'Was he involved in the drugs racket?'

'No. He was clean and so was Trina. It seems that Lorna and Suki were convinced everyone was in on the drugs racket. They'd followed her that night, and Lorna had got in the passenger seat, and when Lorna began to look menacing, she bolted from the car straight into the path of an oncoming car.'

I knew how that felt, and the memories of that awful night came flooding back: Lorna's face like granite, and Suki's sinister smile. I too wanted to jump. I must have paled, because Richard asked, 'Are you OK? Do you want to take a break?'

I took a deep breath. What I wanted was for this to be over.

'What about Victoria?' I asked.

'That Saturday they finished their shift at four p.m. and went straight to the house. Victoria had been drinking and a row broke out. She refused to believe her husband was involved in drug smuggling, and she tried to eject them. Suki lost her temper and smashed her over the head with a hammer.'

'Where did she get the hammer from?'

'Her handbag. There's no doubt murder was her intention. Lorna says she didn't know Suki was carrying a hammer, and she thought they were simply trying to find out if Victoria was involved.'

'Why plant it in Dale Dutchman's place?'

'That was Lorna's idea.'

'How on earth did they manage that?'

'The cleaning-up after the murder took some time. They left before the snow settled, but they didn't go far. They drove away, parked in a lane and waited for hours. Once they thought Dale was asleep, they went back to his place and tried to figure out a way to get in. One of the kitchen windows had a faulty catch, and Suki was slim enough to get in that way.'

'What about Prince? Surely he barked?'

'They threw chocolate in. That kept him quiet, and Dale himself said Prince loved women, but would have barked like mad at a man.'

'What about the roads? Conditions were terrible that night.'

'They managed it by driving miles out of their way. But now we have got witnesses who saw their car.'

'What about Dale's call to the police, which they denied ever occurred?'

'We checked his phone records. He did make the call. It was a computer error – it happens.'

'And poor David?' I asked, my voice hardly

above a whisper. 'Why didn't he meet me in reception?'

'I can answer that,' said the DI. 'He was in touch with the East Midlands police, and he thought he'd make a detour, assuming that Brampton would have left or be leaving for the party. He planned to have a snoop round.'

'That doesn't sound like David,' I said. 'He'd do things by the book.'

'Not this time, unfortunately,' he said solemnly. 'It seems Polly had used her key for the front door, and left by the back door, not bothering to lock it. Inspector Todman, thinking the house was empty, went in and found Suki and Lorna. By this time they'd already killed Brampton. Their pretext for calling was they thought the party was at his place. Suki admits to stabbing him several times. It seems he put up quite a fight, but with Lorna's bulk and Suki's vicious attack, he had no chance. Lorna drove his car with his body in it to the woods, closely followed by Suki in Lorna's car. They went back to the house to clean up the blood. Then David Todman turned up.'

I didn't want to hear any more. My mind was racing. 'Did they think by clearing up the blood they'd get away with it?' I asked.

'They'd got their plane tickets – but not to

Thailand. They planned to go to Spain.'

'Surely Suki wanted to be back with her family?'

'It seems not. She didn't want to carry on being an unpaid nurse to her husband. She'd had a taste of freedom and that's what she wanted.'

'Did they really think they'd get away with it?' I asked, amazed not only at their sheer viciousness, but at their stupidity.

'If they'd stopped at two, they would have done,' he said.

Later that day, with Jasper asleep on my foot, Hubert and I sat in the kitchen drinking yet more tea and churning over events. I still felt responsible for David's death. It seems David had turned up at the back door while Suki and Lorna were cleaning up blood-stains. Taken by surprise, Suki had stabbed him straight in the heart. Death, according to the pathologist, had been more or less instantaneous. The *more or less* worried me. Was that ten seconds? Twenty seconds? A whole minute?

'This time it was him not sticking to the rules,' said Hubert. 'He knew more about the police investigation than you did. Maybe there was a tip-off that Brampton was planning to flee the country. We'll never know.'

'Brampton was supposed to have a spy in the camp, but who it was, I don't know.'

'David told me the security guard was a police informant...'

'He didn't tell me,' I said, feeling disappointed that David hadn't trusted me more.

'He wanted to protect you.'

'I suppose he did in a way,' I murmured. 'The clothes in his overnight bag saved me from dying from hypothermia.'

Hubert didn't come out with any platitudes about time being a healer. He said, 'We'll just go with the flow – shall we?'

'I don't think I can carry on being a PI,' I said. 'Let's face it, I couldn't detect my way out of a paper bag.'

'Now, that's going a bit far, Kate. You try. You understand people...'

'That's rubbish. Did I spot that Suki was an embittered homicidal maniac? Or that Lorna was puppy-like in her devotion? No. I took them at face value. When they didn't show up at the party until late – did warning bells ring? No. I should have looked for them.'

'Where would you have looked?' asked Hubert, patting my hand.

I sighed. I'd wanted everything to be explained and understood, but I knew life wasn't like that, and the sense of failure and guilt wouldn't leave me. And I'd probably lost my last chance of marriage, as too had Hubert.

'Tell you what,' said Hubert. 'We'll go out to eat tonight, and we won't talk about our lost ones or our failures. We'll look to the future.'

'What future?'

'I want a change. I'm seriously thinking of selling the funeral business. We could open a new PI agency – Humberstone and Kinsella. With my organizational skills and your gung-ho approach, we could do well.'

'Kinsella and Humberstone sounds better,' I said.

Maybe I was emotionally drained, but I couldn't think of a single reason to say no.